A ROCKY ROMANCE

A ROCKY ROMANCE

•

Virginia Hart

AVALON BOOKS
THOMAS BOUREGY AND COMPANY, INC.
401 LAFAYETTE STREET
NEW YORK, NEW YORK 10003

c.1

PRINTED IN THE UNITED STATES OF AMERICA
ON ACID-FREE PAPER
BY HADDON CRAFTSMEN, BLOOMSBURG, PENNSYLVANIA

To my mother—also Virginia—whose constant presence at her own typewriter as I was growing up awakened my ambitions; and whose dedication to the cause of helpless creatures inspired me to look beyond myself.

Chapter One

"Ryle Haggard." Dory adjusted the angle of her wide-brimmed hat, as if the midday sun had made her temperature soar, rather than the mental picture she was forming of the new tenant. "What does he look like?"

"Who?" Megan's fingers danced over the keys of her portable word processor without missing a beat.

"The man moving into the rear bungalow. Ryle Haggard."

"Interested?"

Dory worked at sounding convincing. "Just curious."

A silver Volvo swerved into the empty space at the curb. A car door slammed.

"I don't see what good you get out of the sun when you slather on sunblock head to toe." Megan frowned at what she'd written, and jabbed the buttons it took to obliterate it.

"I burn easily. But the sun feels good on my skin." Haggard was a common enough name, Dory mused. In a city the size of Phoenix there could be a dozen Haggards. Still . . . "You showed him the apartment. What does he look like?"

"See for yourself," Megan muttered, as sandaled feet slapped the concrete steps. "Here he comes."

Dory shrank deeper into the chaise longue, hiding her face still more, and allowing only one slate blue eye a glimpse of the lanky, sun-darkened man in ragged cutoffs, who staggered under a stack of cardboard boxes.

That glimpse was enough to make her scalp prickle. Deep-set eyes of a color imperceptible under shaggy dark eyebrows. A tangle of toast brown hair. A nose that had been broken at some time or other. Not from its owner playing football, Dory surmised. While the shoulders were impressively wide, and the arms well muscled, the overall build was too slim to make this Haggard a suitable candidate for the playing field.

No, the slightly off-center proboscis had more reasonably resulted from contact with the fist of someone whose right to privacy he had trampled.

No, it wasn't one of the other Haggards. It was *the* Ryle Haggard, all right. Dory had seen his picture in the paper. Once he'd even managed to get his face on the six o'clock news.

She groaned. Of all the rentals in the city, why did he have to come to this one?

"Hi." Megan wrenched her eyes off the poem she

was composing long enough to wiggle her fingers as the newcomer passed.

The grunt of acknowledgment she received could have been a reciprocated hello or a get lost. *Oops.* Dory pushed her hat back and sprang to her feet as she pictured the walkway leading to bungalow three, and the flower box that ran alongside it.

"Watch out for the—" she began. A crash, a thud, and a surprised outcry cut her warning short.

"The hose," she finished anyway, speeding toward the new arrival, who'd just picked himself up, and now stood with his back to her in a force field of ferocity.

"Is anything broken?" She looked helplessly at the spill of books, dinnerware, and cooking pots. *Please don't let there be a camera in the wreckage,* she begged silently. Not that she cared if he lost some of his equipment. It would be a blessing for society if he did. She just couldn't afford to pay for its replacement.

"No. I always carry broken dishes when I move into a new apartment," he answered through clenched teeth. "What irresponsible joker left the hose hung up here?"

"I did," she admitted, catching her lower lip between her teeth. "The zinnias were withering."

"Zinnias," he repeated, as if flowers were less than dust under his feet.

"Are you okay?" Megan raised her sunglasses to rest on the tousle of her orange-tinted hair. When her question hung in the air unanswered, she went back to her verse.

Inspiration was at work. She'd gone out with an old

flame the night before. Her feelings about him had to be captured for posterity in one of her poems.

"I'm sorry." Dory dropped to her knees and began to gather jagged pieces of what had once been a coffee mug with Bugs Bunny and Elmer Fudd chasing each other around the side.

A squarish hand restrained her. "I'd rather do it myself."

Fine. She didn't particularly want to help him.

"Whatever you say." She brushed off her knees, and tucked a wisp of dark hair under her hat where it belonged.

"Doesn't this place have a gardener?" he said in a growl.

"He only comes on Fridays. When the weather's hot, the flowers need extra attention."

Brown eyes met her slate blue ones. "If that means you make a habit of dragging the hose around the yard, I'll have to watch my step."

On serious inspection, Dory noted, his eyes weren't a deep, honest dark, like the color of black coffee. They were more of a café au lait, with specks and swirls, like the ever-adjusting lens of a camera.

"I said I was sorry."

His expression as he looked down at the clutter said clearly that an apology wasn't nearly enough to compensate him for his trouble.

"I'll be glad to replace anything that's broken."

"Forget it."

In other words, run along. For a person who spent his waking hours invading other people's lives, he was a ridiculously private person.

"Too bad I didn't have my Polaroid," she couldn't resist adding, irritated by his impatient dismissal. "A shot of you falling on your dignity might have been newsworthy."

He jerked his head toward her. "Do I know you?"

Heat crept up her neck. It wasn't her nature to be so outspoken, and, under the circumstances, she'd said too much. He couldn't possibly recognize her. It had been years since all the publicity she and her father had received. Yet she felt a twinge of the old fear.

"I'm sure you don't."

It was true. They'd never met. At—what? Thirty-three or -four—he would have been too young to be among those who had caused so much misery. But she knew what sort of person he had to be: ruthless and self-serving.

He was allowing her answer to click through the divisions and subdivisions of his mind. "This is Sherwood Forest, right? My understanding was that we're one big, happy family here. Like Robin Hood and his Merry Men."

Sherwood Forest. Yuccas and assorted succulents that could withstand blistering summers made up the landscaping, hardly qualifying the circle of cottages for the unlikely name. But Megan had decided on it because her last name was Sherwood.

"Right," Dory said without enthusiasm.

"All for one, and one for all."

"That's the Three Musketeers."

"Same principle."

Was the grin meant to charm her after the surly way he'd spoken? It didn't. Never mind that the flesh-and-blood Haggard was much more attractive than his pictures. All she had to do was remind herself that the appealing outer shell of the man was covering an iron-clad heart.

"Well." She took a step backward.

He took a step forward. "Megan told me the tenants even get together for barbecues and parties."

"Not the kind of parties that would interest you," she shot back with more vehemence than she'd planned.

"You mean no drunken brawls?" He snapped his fingers in feigned disappointment.

"We're just plain folks here. Not a celebrity in the lot." She reconsidered. "At least, not until now."

His small shrug was meant to suggest modesty, and might have worked, if Dory didn't know better. "Megan also tells me that she's a poet," he said.

"She writes poetry." Megan was living proof that there was a definite distinction between writing poetry and being a poet.

"And you?"

"I work with gemstones."

"Sounds interesting."

"It's interesting to me." Where was the conversation going? And how had she allowed it to get started?

"Well." She took another step backward.

He took another forward. "Your name is . . ."

The lighter shade of brown in his eyes hinted at hidden fires, and offered a striking contrast to the thick brush of lashes that had probably helped him get past many a receptionist and into places he didn't belong. They were very nice eyes, actually.

Never mind the man who went with them.

"I'm in unit two." She pointed. That's . . ."

"Next to unit one. But you must have a name."

He was obviously true to his type, since her lack of enthusiasm at meeting him had piqued his interest in her. She recognized him—didn't everyone? But she wasn't enthralled. That represented a challenge.

"Dory," she returned. If she refused to give her name, he'd only be curious, and perhaps dig deeper into her identity.

Or was she blowing things out of proportion? What had happened fifteen years before might have been the most devastating thing that had ever happened to her. But to the vultures who'd played it up in the newspapers and fed on the unhappiness of her and her family, it was yesterday's news.

"Dory what?"

How could she have been stupid enough to spar with him? She should have ignored his belittling attitude and walked away.

"Just Dory. We're one big, happy family here, remember?"

"Dory is short for . . ."

He was probably one of those people who, if given a proper name, insisted on shortening it, and if given a nickname, insisted on using the lengthier version. "Short for nothing." Pandora was unusual enough to give him something to work with.

How she had despised that name when she was small. How she'd been teased by her classmates about her mythical namesake, whose curiosity had unloosed trouble into the world.

"It's a lovely name," her mother had insisted when she complained. "It means 'gifted one.' "

Dory swallowed the ache that still began at the back of her throat when she thought of her mother. Another retreating step took her between two potted acacias.

"Why do I get the impression that you don't like me, Dory?" Ryle asked, not ready to give up so easily.

She set the planters upright, stalling for time. "Maybe you have an inferiority complex."

The fingers of his right hand drummed against his leg. If articles she'd read about body language could be taken seriously, her lack of resounding approval bothered him.

But it was a fair question. "It's your attitude, for one thing. I apologized for leaving the hose in your way, and you chose not to accept."

"A man is entitled to a little snappishness, isn't he, when, as you put it, he falls on his dignity?"

"Maybe." She almost smiled.

"You said 'for one thing.' That means there must be another reason you don't like me."

Had she said that? She'd have to watch herself. This man was a newshound, accustomed to sniffing prospective subjects for his fiendish camera out of nothing.

"It was just an expression."

"Was it?"

"Of course. Well . . ." There was a good ten feet between them now. "Since you won't allow me to undo the damage I've caused, I'll leave you to it."

"An old-fashioned girl," he said, as if to himself. His café au lait eyes narrowed in contemplation.

"Why do you say that?"

"Dory is a nickname for Dorothy. A name from another era." He gestured with one hand. "Then there's that big floppy hat. You don't see many women wearing them nowadays. And . . ."

"And . . ." she prodded.

"And—you're modest."

Was there a hidden insult in the off-base comment? "How did you decide that?"

"You've been sitting by the pool. A legitimate excuse for a beautiful woman to put on a bikini. But you're all covered up."

"Sorry, but you're wrong," she said tightly.

"Meaning you aren't modest?"

Why should she bother to explain about her sun-sensitive skin? "Meaning my name isn't Dorothy."

He raised his shoulders and lowered them. "Two out of three, then."

This time when she retreated, he didn't follow her, but she could feel his eyes, like laser beams, on her all the way. She should have allowed him to believe her name was Dorothy.

" 'A stranger once, a stranger still. Yet in that strangeness, faint hope revives,' " Megan recited with dramatic fervor, as Dory settled onto the poolside chair again.

Ryle Haggard's presence here posed danger. Should she call her father at the shop, Dory wondered, and warn him to be on his toes? No. He didn't need any more reminders of the past.

No one would recognize him now. His dashing mustache was no more. His hair was more gray than black, and he'd put on twenty pounds since his picture had been on the front page of all the newspapers. He was no longer the prominent, well-respected Dr. Zachary T. Brandt, thanks to men like Ryle Haggard. He was just Ted Brandt, semiretired owner of a shop for rock hounds.

Still . . .

"Do you think 'everdark' should be hyphenated? Or do you think punctuation interferes with the flow?" Megan asked.

"Without the hyphen," Dory said, choosing without much thought. "Did you know he was a photographer when you accepted him?"

Haggard was standing on the cement square that served as a porch now, balancing his repacked boxes with one arm as he fumbled with his door key. A tumble of socks, paired into balls, rolled into the soggy flower bed. Dory pretended not to notice.

Dissatisfied, Megan studied what she'd written. "The page looks empty without a hyphen."

"This place is convenient to shopping, buses, everything," Dory persisted. "You can afford to be choosy about tenants. Why did you pick him?"

"Sherwood Forest needs its Robin Hood. Besides, I like to keep a balance of men and women. It makes for better rapport. *Rapport.*" Megan raised one eyebrow. "What a beautiful word. But nothing rhymes with it."

"Weren't other men on the waiting list?"

Megan touched a pensive finger to her lips. "I think he's cute, though, don't you?"

"If by 'cute' you mean clever at turning a situation to his own advantage, yes. He's a photographer."

"And 'photographer' is synonymous with 'ax murderer'?"

"It's synonymous with troublemaker."

Sandaled feet slapped the steps again as Haggard returned to his car for another load of belongings.

"Shouldn't one of us offer him a cold drink?" Megan pondered.

He did look warm. Didn't he have any friends to help him move? Probably not, with his cutthroat personality. It would be interesting to watch him struggle with a stove or refrigerator.

"I don't have any cold drinks," Dory said.

"Ice water then."

"Don't look at me. I'm comfortable."

"Don't be so hard to please. The two of you might hit it off."

"Fat chance."

"If I didn't have a hard-and-fast rule against involvement with new tenants, I'd make a play for him myself. Look at the character in his face. The strong bone structure."

Sherwood Forest's newly declared Robin Hood had allowed a hamper, full of something that clanged and clanked, to slide down his leg and rest on the stoop, where it threatened to topple at any second. He drew a muscled forearm across his face and exhaled.

Dory looked away before he could catch her eye. "You know what I think of his character."

With a sigh, Megan pushed her sunglasses to the top of her head again. "Look, honey, I understand how you feel. But you can't hate all photographers because of what a few did to you over a decade ago. Ryle Haggard wasn't among those who—''

"Shhh!" Dory pressed a warning finger to her lips.

"I used to work in Paradise Mall myself, taking pictures of children on Santa Claus's lap. Does that make me a monster?"

"I don't hate all photographers. Only those who are so eager to be first with a photograph that will shock Mr. and Mrs. John Q. Public, they'll stop at nothing. Only those who have no regard for human suffering or—''

"What makes you think Ryle is that sort?"

"I've seen his work. He's won prizes with it."

"And that's a crime?"

"It is when—'' Dory broke off as the subject of their conversation started back for another armload.

She didn't want to talk about it anymore anyway. The old wounds hadn't healed. They probably never would. But with effort she'd succeeded in closing the door to the nightmarish room that was her past. She wanted it to stay closed—and double padlocked.

The unexpected appearance of Haggard on the scene could mean disaster for her and for her father.

It had been over five years ago that she'd first heard of him. While waiting in line at the supermarket, she'd found her attention drawn to a full-color picture on the cover of a national magazine. It showed the face of a little girl whose father, a race-car driver, had just been involved in a fiery crash.

The picture had been snapped at the moment the car burst into flames, and the horror in the child's eyes had haunted Dory's dreams for months. The photograph was by Ryle Haggard, who happened to be in the right place at the right time. How could he have been so insensitive? How could anyone?

For weeks afterward, Dory had suffered for that little girl. Remembering. In that pale, thin face she'd seen herself when she was twelve. Photographers had taken such pictures of her too, through those terrible months when her father had been wrongly accused—not by the police, but by the press—of helping to end the life of a terminally ill patient. Reporters had held microphones in her face, asking her opinion of her father's guilt or innocence, squeezing words out of her, then twisting those words in print.

But the photographers were worse, getting shots of her at the bus stop and in the park. Not content to wait for her outside school, some had invaded the hallways. In the end, she'd been asked to leave. "For the good of the other students whose classes are being disrupted," her principal had explained.

When those stories had died down, reporters, not content to leave the now-famous Dr. Brandt in peace, discovered that he was seeing his nurse after hours. The dinners the two had together were entirely innocent. They had grown close—as friends, nothing more.

Again reporters and photographers hurled mud at his name. In the end, Dory's mother had filed for divorce.

After that day in the supermarket when Dory saw the tear-wrenching photograph taken at the auto race, she'd found the Haggard name popping up often. Or maybe it was only that she'd become aware of it. He was always first on the scene of anything important. He always managed to capture the humor, the poignancy, the shock of the given situation. A car chase. A plane crash. A mine cave-in.

"I think you should give him a chance to prove himself before you make a judgment," Megan was saying. "But if you feel you can't, at least don't start a feud. I like peace and tranquillity. Anything else shatters my creative spirit. Got it?"

"Got it," Dory repeated, closing her eyes.

"I came from a family with five kids," Megan went on. "At any given time, somebody was screaming at somebody. If that wasn't bad enough, the cracker-box flat we lived in had paper-thin walls. One neighbor would say something. Another would take offense. Everybody would take sides against everybody else. When I grew up, I swore to myself I would have harmony at all costs."

Dory had heard the story many times before. "I understand," she said.

"Good." Her speech made, Megan again turned her attention to the miniature screen. "Is there such a word as 'forbidable'?"

"I don't know."

"There is now." The rose-lacquered fingertips began to tap-dance across the keys of the word processor again.

Harmony at all costs.

Dory sighed and concentrated on the clickety-clack of poetic genius at work, hoping to push away the threatening swirl of ugly memories.

Megan was the one person in her present she had

allowed a glimpse of her past. For the last five years the girl had been there when Dory needed a friend. Megan had been understanding and supportive.

Dory had no intention of making trouble. She'd simply stay out of Haggard's way and pray that he had the good sense to stay out of hers.

Chapter Two

The penny rolled off the kitchen table and shivered to a stop, and Dory groaned. Tails would have meant she cooked dinner. Heads assigned her to laundry duty. "Why do you always win the toss?"

A grin creased her father's face. "The luck of the Irish."

"Quite a coincidence. You like nothing better than throwing together a pot of stew when you come back from one of your rock hunts."

"Throwing together?" He pretended to feel hurt. "Not an apt assessment of my culinary skills."

"And you detest the new washing machine."

"Too many buttons." His skin was red from the weekend of desert sun.

"Did you remember to put on sunblock?" she asked, knowing the answer already.

He wasn't listening. He'd already opened the fridge and was contemplating what would grace his pot. Was it her imagination or was there more gray in his dark hair than there had been before?

"Messy, messy." She dumped the contents of his duffel bag into the clothes basket. "What'd you do? Roll in the dirt?"

"It's not a tea party out there." He considered a bottle of Tabasco sauce, then put it back again.

Evidently Wilda was coming to dinner. He hadn't yet educated her palate to the joys of cayenne pepper. Ted had been seeing Wilda Moffet for almost two years now. They'd met at the fairgrounds, where he ran a booth displaying wares from the Rock Place and she had a quilt entered at the craft show. Now that quilt covered Ted's bed, and a fish he'd carved from jade graced her mantelpiece.

She was a pretty blond woman, with a sunny disposition and a mother-hen attitude toward him, despite the fact that she was twelve years younger. Dory would have imagined her fussing would drive Ted up a wall. Somehow it didn't, or if it did, he hid it well.

Dory liked her too. Wilda's exuberance for life was contagious and admirable. After putting in an eight-hour day at the office, she still had enthusiasm for quilting and making cross-stitch samplers for friends. Her desserts were a feast for the eyes as well as the palate. But single-handedly she'd been responsible for the fifteen pounds Ted needed to lose.

"Men work hard and need to eat," was always her chirped reply to Dory's protests.

Dory took the box of detergent out of the cabinet

under the sink. "I waxed the kitchen floor last night. Try not to let your creativity get away from you."

"Wilda'll help you with the cleanup." Ted poured oil in the bottom of his favorite iron pot and set the stove burner on low.

"Help me? You're the cook. The cleanup is yours." Ducking out quickly, so she wouldn't hear his retort, she let the screen door slam behind her. Actually she didn't mind doing laundry. A bowl of her father's spicy stew sounded good, though she'd hoped they'd be alone that night. They needed to talk about the new and revolting development—Ryle Haggard.

As she approached the laundry room, she didn't hear any chugging or spinning. Maybe she'd be lucky. Megan had only one washer and one dryer, and on weekends Dory usually she had to wait for a machine.

Suspicion washed over her and she set her clothes basket down. Another sound came from the storage room. Something was being dragged across the cement floor, and the door was partly open.

Megan was the only other person who had a key, and Dory couldn't imagine what she'd be doing to make such noises. Maybe it was Harry. Easygoing and eager to please, Harry Paige, the tenant from unit 5, and Megan's wanna-be beau, was easy for her to press into service.

Gingerly, Dory inched the door open.

It wasn't Megan or Harry. It was Ryle, and he'd been busy. Everything that had been on the shelves was on the floor, and he had her trunk and footlocker in the middle of the room.

"Hey." Driving back her fear of discovery, she pointed. "Those are mine."

"Then you're the person I want to see." As it had at their last meeting, a thatch of nut brown hair fell in fetching disarray over his forehead. A roguish smile said he expected her to be glad to see him too.

She clenched and unclenched her fists, teetering between anxiety and fury. "You didn't open them?"

"Why would I?"

Foolish question in the light of his making a profession out of snooping. "I can think of a number of reasons."

"What've you got inside, atomic secrets?"

"Don't you have a cache of personal things you'd rather not have anyone see?"

He twisted his mouth to one side. "Pictures of myself when I thought a ponytail was cool?"

Dory didn't crack a smile. The locks were still in place. He couldn't have rifled through her belongings—yet.

He reached for a can of root beer he'd set on the windowsill and took a swig. "I've been trying to figure out what to do with them. They're in my way."

In his way? Did he hope to store something in here too? He couldn't. Megan would never agree to it.

"I want everything exactly where it was. Not in a dusty corner where I can't get at it. I'll thank you to"—she gestured widely—"to put it back, and clear out."

"There won't be any dusty corners when I get through." He glanced around with a show of pride. A broom leaned against the wall, and dust lay in a neat pile in the middle of the floor. A streak of black ran down one prominent cheekbone. His shirt was missing a button, and the hem of his no-color jeans was ragged.

Perversely, it ruffled her further that even disheveled he could look so appealing—from his chiseled features to the winsome smile that belied the aura of self-confidence he exuded. Too bad those head-turning good looks were wasted on someone with Ryle's basic makeup.

"When you get through doing what?"

"You're standing in the middle of my darkroom."

This was all she needed. "Why would you need a darkroom?"

He waited a good five seconds to answer, wanting to emphasize the stupidity of her question. "I'm a photographer."

"Many professional photographers don't process their own pictures. They use a lab."

"Some do. I prefer to be in control."

"That doesn't surprise me."

"So . . ." He looked at his broom pointedly. "If you let me know where you want your footlockers, I'll move them for you."

"As I said, I don't want them moved anywhere."

One dark eyebrow peaked. "I have plans for every inch of space. My file cabinets will need most of the wall."

Dory raised an eyebrow back at him. "Megan and I have a standing arrangement."

"When I talked to her yesterday, she said there'd be no problem." His good nature was visibly slipping.

"She was wrong." Seething inside, Dory tapped her foot on the floor. "There are two windows in here. Darkrooms can't have windows."

"I can deal with windows." He stared at her tapping foot. "I didn't realize I'd be evicting you."

"We'll see who evicts who." She inhaled sharply and stalked out the door.

"Hey . . ."

"In the meantime," she yelled back, "don't touch my trunks. I don't want anything broken."

"Come in the house." Harry was wearing a tie-dyed T-shirt and knee-length shorts in eye-popping colors. "What can we do for you, pretty lady?"

Dory pushed past, her resentment at Ryle's presumption spilling onto him. If Harry and Ryle hadn't been friends, Ryle wouldn't have heard about the vacancy, and wouldn't be here.

Megan was making salad dressing from a packet of seasoning. The shades were drawn, and fat silver candles decorated the table as well as the mantelpiece, and every other available surface.

"It's that . . . that . . ." Dory couldn't force herself to pronounce his name. "That photographer you let invade our domain."

"Remember our little talk?" Megan hit the bottom of the foil packet to dislodge the last granule of seasoning. "Peace at all costs?"

"Tell Robin Hood about it." Dory threw one arm out to the side. "He's tearing the place apart."

"He's what?" Megan handed Harry the bottle. "Would you mind using some muscle to shake this?"

"Ryle's setting up his darkroom," Harry explained, swinging the crystal cruet from one shoulder to the other in a kind of South American rhythm as he complied with Megan's request.

"Not in the storage room, he isn't." Dory turned back to her friend. "He tried to tell me he has your permission."

"As a matter of fact, he has." Megan plucked a crouton out of the bowl and popped it into her mouth. "You asked to use it a long time ago. I figured you'd have everything disposed of by now."

"Megan." Dory edged closer, trying to signal with facial contortions that she didn't care to discuss the contents of her trunks in front of an outsider—especially an outsider like Harry, who had the enemy's ear. "Things I've stored away are priceless to me. I thought you understood."

"I meant to tell you about the arrangement with Ryle, but it slipped my mind."

"How could you?"

"He offered good hard cash." Megan circled the fingers of one hand against its thumb. "And I need the money."

Dory crossed her arms and uncrossed them. What answer did she have to that? Because Megan didn't have a regular job, her finances were strained. Not only did she want to be on the premises to keep an eye on her apartments, there was her poetry. Though she was a realist in most ways, she allowed herself the dream that someday her talent would be recognized. Her days would be spent signing her poetry books, and her nights giving readings before rapt audiences.

In the meantime, she worked as an office temp—when and if she felt like it.

"I doubt Ryle would be bent out of shape if you kept your junk to one side." Harry's grin showed a gap between his two front teeth, making him look about sixteen. "Say pretty please."

Dory glared at him. That would be the day.

"How about under the shelves in the laundry room?" Megan suggested.

"Everyone would have access to it."

"What do you keep in there anyway?" Harry asked, handing the bottle back to Megan.

"Things that are important to me—only me."

Megan shrugged. "Couldn't you boil the contents down enough to fit in the footlocker alone, and stow it in the back of your closet?"

And have her father notice it, and guess that she'd saved so many remnants of the past? Recognizing defeat, Dory backed toward the door. "Never mind, it isn't your problem. Have a lovely dinner."

"Care to join us?" Megan asked.

"Yeah, why not?" Harry tried to look enthusiastic about Dory staying, but failed miserably. Undoubtedly he'd envisioned a romantic dinner for two—a possibility that, Dory could have informed him, might come about if he didn't wear his sun-streaked blond hair surfer-style. It only emphasized the difference in his and Megan's ages.

"Thanks," Dory said. "But my father's throwing together one of his famous stews."

So Ryle had won, she steamed silently, deciding to take the long way around the pool to avoid another encounter with him. Let him learn about his victory on his own. Distracted by her thoughts, she didn't notice him waiting outside and literally ran into him.

''Ouch.'' He groaned, holding a hand over his face as if the collision had injured him.

She didn't react. ''You were eavesdropping?''

''Would I do that?'' He shrugged. ''I knew what Megan's answer would be.''

''So now you want to crow?'' She planted her hands on her hips. ''Go ahead. I have a few seconds.''

His scowl pulled his eyebrows together as if they were one. ''As I tried to say before you went running off, we can talk this over.''

''I can't afford to outbid you on the space.'' She stepped past him.

''It isn't a question of outbidding,'' he called after her. ''It doesn't make sense to keep an entire room vacant for six square feet of trunk. Dory . . .''

She pretended not to hear.

Wilda arrived half an hour later. The woman had been to the beauty salon, and her hair was a short cap of silvery blond curls. ''Let's not do candles tonight,'' she said as Dory started to touch a match to one of the wicks. ''Everything's pretty enough, with the blue linen cloth and thick blue soup mugs, don't you think?''

''A dinner's more festive by candlelight,'' Dory reasoned, fighting back irritation. The warm, comforting glow she'd felt in Megan's apartment with flickering flames all about made the idea seem like a good one. Tonight she needed all the warmth and comfort she could get.

"Ted likes to see what he's eating. I learned a long time ago that men . . ." A shuffle of footsteps outside the front door and three deafening thumps interrupted Wilda, and her attention whipped to the sound. "Are either of you expecting company?"

Ted shrugged. "Not me. But I'll get it."

"Be careful. It sounds like the big, bad wolf."

"Fine. He can join us for dinner. There's plenty."

"You know how men are about candles," Wilda whispered, continuing her earlier objection as the pounding came again, and Ted loped over to answer. "It's only we women who think a dim atmosphere is romantic."

Before Dory could argue the point, a hostile voice alerted her that trouble was afoot.

"Don't give me that hooey," a man bellowed. "I've been around long enough to know a brush-off when I hear one."

"I'm sorry." Ted's voice was strained.

"Sorry doesn't get it, buster. We had a deal and I promised my kids. They've been looking forward to the trip."

"I sent your check back."

"I don't want your crummy check. Do I have to go to the Better Business Bureau?"

"Do what you have to do," Ted said calmly. "Now if you don't mind, my daughter and I were about to sit down to dinner."

"Not so fast." The big man shoved the door open wider with his foot, and Dory could see him clearly.

His meaty face was florid, and the sleeves of his T-shirt were rolled up to show tattooed biceps. A boy of about sixteen, not as tall, but nearly as bulky, stood next to him.

"You got something against me personally?" the man snarled.

"I explained in my letter," Ted said. "Didn't you get it?"

"I'm calling the police." Dory started for the telephone.

"Not yet," Wilda whispered, tugging at her sleeve. "Ted will think you don't trust him to handle the situation."

"This isn't the OK Corral. I'd rather have him think that than see him hurt." Still Dory hesitated, wondering if it might not be preferable to go over and stand beside her father as backup.

"Is everything okay here?" Ryle asked, appearing suddenly, tilting the balance of hostility.

Relieved, Dory drew a shaky breath. For once, she was actually glad to see him.

"Hey, the two of us are talking," the intruder said, quieter about his anger now. "We got business to discuss."

"We don't have anything more to talk about," Ted insisted. "I can give you a list of phone numbers. People who might be willing to take your group out."

"Forget it." The man favored Ryle with a glare that was designed to intimidate, decided it was useless, and stalked off, trailed by his son. "I got friends at City Hall."

"Think he'll be back?" Ryle's hair looked shower-damp. He'd changed into a crisp white shirt with the sleeves rolled up to the elbows, and khaki slacks. He smelled of soap and something deliciously spicy.

"I doubt it." Ted followed his gaze to the street, where the unwelcome visitors had climbed into an old Dodge truck and were shooting away from the curb. "He's not a bad sort."

"Not a bad sort?" Dory echoed. "Honestly, Dad, you'd give Attila the Hun a good character reference."

"He's had one drink too many. Which was one of the problems I had with him. Drinking and rock hunts don't mix."

"I'm Ryle Haggard." Ryle stuck out one squarish hand to Ted.

"The new tenant?"

"That's me. I met your daughter this morning." Ryle looked at Dory and nodded. "Wilda and I ran into each other a few minutes ago."

"I dropped my car keys in the gutter," Wilda explained with a small giggle. "Ryle retrieved them for me. This is his night for rescues."

"I don't think it qualified as a rescue," Dory said.

"It did to me." Wilda tittered. "My hands were full."

"I'm grateful you came along when you did," Ted said. "Ott belabors a point when he's had a few, and we might have been standing here for an hour. Now that we know each other, Ryle, want to join us for dinner?"

"Mr. Haggard already has plans, Dad," Dory said quickly—too quickly. "That is, I'm sure he does."

Ryle's eyes met hers. "I was about to pop something in the microwave."

"Humph! Microwaves are a super invention." As if it were all settled, Wilda teetered to the china cabinet on her high heels to take out another place setting. "For heating leftovers, that is. But nothing cooked in one qualifies as dinner. Sit down, or you'll hurt Ted's feelings. He cooked tonight, and you're in for a treat."

"You're putting him on the spot," Dory tried again.

"A spot I don't mind being in," Ryle said jovially. "It smells fantastic."

"Sit here." Wilda circled the table to touch the back of one of the chairs, then another. "You here, Dory. "That'll be boy, girl, boy, girl. Perfect."

Making no comment, Dory willed a bland expression onto her face as she accepted her assigned seat. Wilda and her take-charge habit. Dory hadn't had a chance yet to explain to her father about Ryle.

Ted held his spoon aloft until the others had tasted his masterpiece and made appropriate sounds of appreciation. "Need salt or pepper? Tabasco? Anything?"

"It's superb like it is." Ryle gave a thumbs-up.

Wilda rolled her eyes ceilingward. "Absolutely wonderful."

Having made several exceptional finds on his latest trip, and in a better-than-average mood, Ted explained about Harvey Ott, the man who'd gone away mad, and the nightmarish weekend he'd had when he took the Otts rock hunting a few weeks before.

His boys, three of them, one only nine, scrambled up hills without watching where they were going.

They strewed pop cans and potato chip bags everywhere, which was bad enough in itself because Ted was a fanatic about leaving the land the way he found it.

"The next day was worse. I kept warning about the dangers of shallow mines underfoot. But they wouldn't listen, until the oldest boy came near to being buried in falling debris. The only thing that got me through was a promise I made myself not to take them again."

"That's your line?" Ryle asked. "You supervise amateur prospectors?"

"Sometimes. Mostly I run the Rock Place, a shop at Dearborn and Kenneth."

"You deal in gemstones?"

"And petrified wood. I contribute to a few journals, and take my stuff to mineral and gem shows, where I sell and trade. But my daughter's the artist. Her talent brings in the customers."

"Dory works with you?"

Ted nodded. "She makes jewelry. I put together clocks, picture frames, and such, for those who want to display what they've found in the form of usable objects."

"She's an extremely talented young woman." Wilda beamed at Dory. "Barely out of pinafores, she already has a degree from the Institute of Gemology. Besides that, she teaches classes in jewelry making."

Dory cringed. Wilda was trying to be nice, but at twenty-seven, Dory was too old to be considered "barely out of pinafores."

"A family business." Ryle broke a biscuit in half and buttered it lavishly. "That's the way to go."

"Did you follow in your father's footsteps?" Dory asked sweetly, doubting that he was a second-generation cameraman. "Is he a photographer too?"

"Nope. He's a plumber."

That bit of news should have alerted Ted to the danger of their guest, but he didn't appear to notice the key word *photographer*.

"You don't know your way around pipes and plungers then?" Dory pressed on.

"Actually I do." Ryle stopped with the biscuit halfway to his mouth. "Pop insisted on my sister and I learning the basics, and we worked after school. Why? Do you have a leaky faucet?"

"No."

"A clogged drain?"

She lowered her gaze to her bowl. "I was only curious."

A practiced interviewer, Ryle managed to finish two helpings of stew, as well as three of Wilda's biscuits, all the while juggling a probing conversation.

He was born in Philadelphia, he replied to the questions Dory asked in self-defense, but was reared in Chicago. He'd come to Phoenix about a year and a half ago to start a job that didn't pan out. But he'd stayed on as a freelancer.

"I hated this part of the country on sight. Hemmed in on all sides by mountains. And where were the brilliant greens and reds and shades in between? Here everything was muted by glare and sand. It was like looking at the world through a gauze curtain."

"But you don't feel that way anymore?" Wilda asked.

"I've grown to love it. The warm browns and tans. The never-ending turquoise sky the brochures brag about. I began to realize that the Midwest isn't better. It's just different."

"But you miss the change of seasons, don't you?" Dory tried.

He nodded. "Perpetual sunshine takes getting used to."

"You'll get used to it," Wilda assured him. "Believe me, I know. I withstood twenty years of Illinois winters before I came here."

"But you might be going home soon?" Dory tried not to sound too hopeful.

"I'm not sure where home is anymore." Ryle dropped his napkin on the table next to his plate. "This past week I got a job offer at *Palestra* magazine in San Francisco. The money's great, and I'd have a free hand. But it's a tough decision to make."

"Some people think of San Francisco as being the most exciting city in the world. Why wouldn't you accept this dream offer?"

"I need to give the headman an answer within the month, and to be honest, I don't want to yank up roots again without giving it a lot of thought."

"What is it they say about the worst regrets involving a road not taken?" Dory persisted.

"Twenty-six days can fly by mighty quick." His half smile warned that she was being too obvious. "As I said, I have some hard thinking to do."

If he'd carried it as far as counting the days until

he had to decide—twenty-six—that meant he was seriously considering the offer. It also meant she could cross the days off on a calendar until she and her father could breathe easy again.

"You're right to move slowly. You spend a third of your life at work." Wilda went on about her own job, and how much she loved it. "I hope it doesn't sound like bragging when I say I get more fan mail than anybody else on my floor."

Because she was the gatherer of social tidbits for the "In and Around Town" section of a local newspaper, people naturally wrote to her hoping to see their names in print. But Dory didn't remark on it.

"At times a little bragging is appropriate," Ted said. "For instance, I'm feeling ten feet tall about a chunk of jasper I'm working on now. If you're interested, Ryle, I'll show you after dinner."

"What are you making?"

"A simple paperweight. But it's a beauty. You don't often come across a stone with as much character as this one."

Her father was talking too much. Dory had never seen anyone able to draw him out the way Ryle was doing. It had to be stopped.

But how?

"You've got to admit," Ted said, in answer to a question about the cost of equipment needed in working with gemstones, "ancient people did impressive work with only sticks, mud, and sand."

"True enough."

"When I was a kid, I made a number of fair pieces with only a hacksaw blade. When I had them the way

I wanted, I'd rub them smooth on the sidewalk in front of our house.''

"Your parents didn't encourage you in your craft?" Ryle asked.

Ted snorted. "I come from a long line of doctors. Any ambition that didn't include a medical degree was out of the question."

"Well, now." Needing to cut that particular topic off at the pass, Dory scraped her chair back and popped up. "I'll fix coffee."

"Fine," Ted said.

"Why don't you tell Ryle about the special properties of fire agate?" she said, fearing that when she left the room, the story about her doctor grandfather and his medical ambitions for his only son might end in unplanned revelation. "It's fascinating. The iridescence comes from iron oxide caught between the layers. Tell him how careful you have to be when you work with it."

"I think you already told him." Ted shot her a quizzical look before turning his attention back to Ryle. "When it comes down to it, a beginner is better off with crude equipment. Mistakes can't happen as fast. He can stop before damage is too extensive."

"I'll get that coffee," Dory said, grateful that he'd veered temporarily, at least, off the subject of his parents' disapproval.

Now she had to hurry.

Chapter Three

Counting to twenty, Dory pressed her palms to the cool blue tiles of the counter. Thirteen, fourteen. The copper bottoms of the pans that hung on a row of hooks to her left had never looked so gleaming before Wilda came into their life. The chrome stovetop had never sparkled as it did now.

Seventeen, eighteen. What were Ted and Ryle talking about now? Nineteen, twenty.

She pushed the door to the dining room open and called, "Dad, I could use your help in the kitchen."

She wouldn't have time to tell him much. She'd only make him aware of possible motives behind Ryle's seemingly innocent questions.

To her frustration, her summons brought not Ted, but Wilda. "The boys are talking." The woman's

34

smile made her eyes crinkle. "I thought I could help with whatever it is you need."

"The boys have done plenty of talking already," Dory said through clenched teeth.

Looking crushed, Wilda blinked. "If you need Ted, I'll get him."

"No, no. It's nothing," Dory managed, miffed at herself for hurting the woman's feelings. "I wanted him to reach on that top shelf for the . . . the new jar of coffee creamer. But I noticed we have some left."

"Is everything all right?"

Dory hadn't thought her anxiety was so obvious. "I'm not fond of Mr. Haggard. He's so . . . pushy."

"He seems very nice to me. Maybe you met him at an off moment."

"Ryle has nothing but off moments."

"Really?" The woman wasn't convinced. "If you do the coffee, honey, I'll cut the cheesecake."

So that was what was in the covered cake dish. "Make the slices thin, won't you? It's terribly rich."

"Cheesecake is Ted's favorite dessert. Let him splurge this one night."

And every other night when Wilda toddled over with a rich dessert, Dory thought. For now, though, she was too preoccupied to discuss calorie count. Collecting necessary cups and saucers too speedily, she almost dropped the tray.

Wilda caught it just in time. "Hard day at the shop?"

"I didn't go in today. I'm working at home on that

bracelet for my Kingman customer. If she likes it, I might be able to sell to her more regularly.''

"You're pushing yourself too hard."

"Maybe." Dory turned her attention to the task at hand and hoped her companion would do the same.

"Onyx carves easily, so you might think it's a good choice for a beginner," Ted was saying when Dory backed through the door with the coffee, trailed by Wilda, who'd cut the cheesecake into slices three times the thickness they should have been. "But it chips easily.''

Ryle pressed a hand to his middle in protest when he spied the strawberry-topped dessert. "I couldn't eat another bite.''

"There's always room for dessert." Wilda set his dish in front of him.

"How can I resist? It looks a lot more tempting than the one we featured in that cookbook spread last week.''

"Thank you, sir." Wilda executed a small curtsy.

Ryle took a spoonful, and noisily kissed the tips of his fingers in a gesture of appreciation. "Even better than it looks.''

Wilda waited until the compliments had circled the table. "So, everybody, dig in.''

"If you don't mind, Ted," Ryle said, after a few minutes of silence as they ate, "I'd like to tag along on one of those rock hunts.''

"I don't see why not," Ted said.

"When I was a kid I used to dream about discovering a lost gold mine.''

"That's not unusual," Dory assured him, feeling

the conversation getting out of hand again. "All children go through that stage. In between wanting to be a cowboy and a movie star."

"Two ambitions I can't say I ever contemplated." Ryle accepted the coffee cup Wilda offered, but refused cream and sugar. "There's a good story in that shop of yours, Ted. A human-interest piece."

"Why should there be?" Dory interrupted again. "In Phoenix there's a rock shop on every corner."

"Hey. Whose side are you on?" Ted countered. "The Rock Place stands out."

"Ryle will only be disappointed when he doesn't find chunks of gold scattered all over the desert floor."

"What makes you think I expect that?" Ryle wanted to know.

"He doesn't realize," she continued, as if she hadn't heard his question, "that most of the time a prospector doesn't find enough to pay for the gas money it takes to drive to the field. Everything's been picked over."

"Not so," Ted argued. "If you don't do well on your first outing, there's always a next time."

"Hope springs eternal," Wilda chirped.

"The prospector's motto," Dory said in a growl, unhappy about Ryle's interest in the store.

Had Megan let something slip about the Brandt background? The girl always spent time with new applicants, wanting to make sure they fit into her "family" before she signed them up. Tricky as Ryle was, he could easily have turned the tables and gleaned information as well.

Just in case, Dory continued to jump at each gap in

the conversation, not only describing her current project in more detail than anyone cared to hear, but drawing their guest out enough about his early life to write his biography.

His widowed mother was living in Chicago, and still ran the plumbing business with hired help. He had one sister, in Louisville, Kentucky. She'd made him an uncle of twin girls.

"While I think about it," he said suddenly, turning his attention to Dory again, after sending a walletful of baby pictures around the table, "I want to apologize again for displacing you. We can work something out."

"How did you displace her?" Wilda wanted to know. "What happened?"

"Nothing. Everything's settled." This was all Dory needed. Ted knew nothing about the trunk. He had no idea she had rescued so much of what he'd thrown out years before, when constant reminders of happier times were too much for him to bear.

"What's settled?" he wanted to know.

"Nothing important. Ryle and I had a discussion earlier in the storage room."

"What were you doing in the storage room?" Ted looked at her over the top of his coffee cup.

"He's turning it into a darkroom. To process the pictures he takes." Dory waited for her comment to sink in. "Some of those pictures are too newsworthy to trust to an ordinary lab."

Ryle stopped with his fork an inch from his mouth. "It's not that exactly."

"Uh-oh." Dory glanced at the wall clock behind

her father's chair, and popped to her feet again. "I hate to break up the party, but time is getting away from us. Remember, Dad, you plan to open early tomorrow morning."

"I do?"

"You know how grouchy you are if you don't have your eight hours' sleep. Why don't you walk Wilda home, and I'll show Ryle the bracelet I'm making?"

Wilda checked her watch, no doubt noticing that it was earlier than she usually left. She lived only two streets away and seldom brought her car, wanting to use the trek back and forth as exercise. "I have to do the dishes first."

"You've already spent enough time in the kitchen, preparing that delectable cheesecake. Ryle and I didn't have a hand in the meal, so it's only fair that we do KP duty." Dory made a point of not looking at Ryle, but she could sense his surprise at hearing her volunteer his services.

"Well . . ." Wilda's vacant expression remained for many long moments. Then as if a lightbulb had gone off over her head, she exchanged I-get-it glances with Ted. "If you're sure you don't mind. I have to be at work early tomorrow too. We're having a party for a girl who's expecting a baby, and I'm in charge. Are you ready to go, Ted?"

Ted took another drink of coffee before rising. "If you are."

She'd been obvious, Dory realized, after he and Wilda had gone. It would seem to everyone, especially Ryle, that she'd manipulated things to be alone with him. But it couldn't be helped.

Feeling less pressured when it was only the two of them, she lapsed into silence. If he was bored with her company, maybe he'd leave before Ted returned. She worked quietly, washing dishes as he dried them. If he minded helping out, he didn't let on, except that he was quiet too, speaking only to ask what went in which drawer or cabinet.

As promised, after they were finished with the dishes, she showed him the bracelet—delicate strands of gold twisted around carnelian droplets, as if they were bunches of grapes. Then she brought out a mosaic she'd already finished for another customer. On an eleven-by-fourteen piece of wood, she'd created a picture with polished gemstones.

"These were all found by my customer's daughter. They're not gem quality, but arranged to look like flowers in a vase, I think they're effective."

Ryle registered polite appreciation, but his thoughts were traveling on a different track. "I keep thinking of how protective you are of those old trunks," he said as they returned to the living room.

"I don't know what you mean."

"You turned pale when you saw them in the middle of the floor."

"I didn't turn pale. I'm naturally that way."

"There's pale, and then there's *pale*." He drew the word out. "What do you really keep in it? Old love letters?"

He was teasing, hoping to lighten the prevailing mood. She tried not to read more into his question. "The jumble defies categorization. Among other things there are letters, yes."

Some were from her mother, written after her move to Florida, begging Dory to come live with her and her new husband.

"Zach has made such a mess of his life," the woman had written. "Don't let him make a mess of yours too."

"Letters tied in blue satin ribbons?" Ryle asked.

"Why would you think that?"

"I don't, actually." His eyes glittered with humor. "You don't fit the stereotype."

"You don't know enough about me to decide if I do."

"It wasn't meant as an insult." He looked at the couch, as if he expected to stay. "I still think the shop—and the idea behind it—would make an interesting piece. Father and daughter working together."

Didn't he ever give up, or was he one of those men who thought bickering was the only way to keep up a conversation with a woman? "The answer is still no."

His jaw squared. "Publicity would be good for the business."

"Dad isn't a publicity hound." She took several steps toward the front door. "It was nice having you, Ryle. Thank you for helping in the kitchen."

"I gather you want me to leave."

She gestured limply. "As long as we're finished here."

"We aren't." His voice had taken on an edge. He crossed to the couch, sat down, and patted a cushion beside him. "Sit, Dory. You keep taking jabs at me. I want to know why."

Deciding that humoring him would be the quickest way to usher him out the door, she did as he asked.

"As I see it, there has to be a plausible reason for your animosity." He touched one index finger to the other in an attitude of counting off. "Possibility A, you believe in reincarnation, and we were bitter enemies in a former life."

She groaned at his nonsense. "Possibility B has to be better."

"Possibility B, I remind you of someone you used to know in this life, and didn't like."

As if she had ever met anyone remotely like Ryle Haggard. "Is there a C?"

"C, you've been hurt by someone in the past, and now you hate all men."

"This is multiple choice, and I'm supposed to pick one?"

"I'll do the picking, after I know you better."

"What makes you believe you will?"

When he reached out casually, she assumed it was to smooth a displaced lock of hair off her forehead. Silky fine, and always a trial to keep in place, it was flyaway tonight. The stress of the last two hours—and the proximity of the last two minutes—had made her uncomfortably warm.

If that was his plan, it changed when his finger grazed her cheekbone. His other hand came into play too, and before she had time for a defensive move, it was at her back. His lips caught hers, softly, sweetly, yet with a shattering sense of delight.

Calling on every inch of her determination, she

pulled back. ''What was that for?'' she whispered, too breathless to sound indignant.

''It was meant to eliminate choice C,'' he said perfunctorily. ''It did. You definitely aren't a man-hater.''

The kiss was an experiment? Forcing back her outrage, she moved from sitting to standing. ''You can't fathom that anyone would dislike you for yourself.''

''Not at first sight. You began firing shots from moment one.''

Too miffed to engage in any more banter, she strode to the door and grasped the knob so hard she felt her knuckles turn white. Why bother with gentle hints when dealing with somebody too dense to appreciate them? ''Will you please go?''

''This man in your past . . .''

''This mystery man you've conjured up . . .''

''The one who hurt you. Did he look anything like me?'' He showed her first one profile, then the other.

''Good night, Ryle.''

''Good night, Dory.'' He walked over to where she stood and gave her a goofy grin it was impossible not to return. His eyes were liquid chocolate. ''Maybe we should recheck choice C, to be sure.''

''Good night, Ryle,'' she repeated.

For a fraction of a moment, she thought he would kiss her again. The movement of his mouth suggested that he was tasting her lips already. To her chagrin, a part of her hoped it would happen. It didn't. He walked past her, not looking back.

When she closed the door, she stood with her back against it for many long moments, listening to his retreating footsteps, and wondering why it took her heart so long to resume its normal pattern.

As she moved through the apartment, putting things away, she couldn't stop thinking about the tidal wave of emotions she'd experienced that night. Ryle had succeeded in unsettling her as no one had unsettled her before, because she'd been totally unprepared for the alarming events of the day.

He wouldn't succeed again.

When Ted returned half an hour later, she was able to explain her worries at last. "Ryle is more than an ordinary photographer. He's won awards for ferreting out shocking stories about innocent people."

"So he's good at his job." Ted opened the refrigerator and put a jar on the top shelf. "Wilda gave me some homemade jam. A gift from one of her readers."

"We need to discourage any attempts on his part to get friendly. To keep our distance."

"You didn't exactly distance yourself from him tonight." Ted chuckled.

"I had to be sociable or he might have suspected something."

"I like him." Ted took out a carton of milk and poured half a glass. "He's good company."

Dory opened a cabinet and checked the label on one of the medicine bottles. "That's the problem. He's developed an ability to put people at ease. When they aren't prepared—wham—he leaps out at them."

Ted accepted the vitamin pill she handed him, and swallowed it with the milk. "I look at lot different than I did in the old days, baby. You could put my picture in the post office and nobody would recognize me.''

''Fifteen years is not all that long. How can you be sure?''

''Take my word for it.'' He put his glass in the sink and ran water in it. ''How did the car run today?''

It was difficult to know for sure—his face didn't give away much of what he was thinking—but she couldn't help but wonder if he was as concerned about discovery as she was, and only trying to soft-pedal his fears for her sake.

''A little trouble starting, as usual,'' she said, going along with his change of subject.

''You ought to get a new one.''

''Maybe if Lorraine likes these bracelets, and starts ordering from me on a regular basis, I'll have enough money to swing something.'' Lorraine Frye, proprietor of the Vanishing American in Kingman had a number of other outlets for Dory's work in Los Angeles, Santa Barbara, and San Francisco.

''You could swing it now.''

''If absolutely necessary.'' Keeping a healthy bank account to deal with emergencies was more important than new wheels.

''My guess is, it'll be necessary mighty soon.'' Ted hesitated, signaling that there was more on his mind. ''Wilda thinks you don't like her.''

''What is there not to like?''

He didn't answer immediately. ''Could be more depth to her than you realize. She works for a news-paper. Why doesn't she arouse your suspicions?''

Dory hooted. "A column in a local newspaper isn't exactly 'Sixty Minutes.' "

"She knows lots of people."

"People who give parties and want to see their names in the paper. There's a huge difference between Wilda and Ryle. He has cutthroat, unstoppable ambitions."

Ted's laugh was dry. "Not making snap judgments, are you, baby?"

It wouldn't have been a good idea for her to explain about the photograph of the little girl that had tugged at her heart. Ted would have known she was likening the child's tragedy to her own and would have felt hurt.

"He has an ugly reputation."

"Is that so?" He was humoring her, waiting for her reaction to what he'd said moments before.

Dory pressed her lips together. "I'll be more friendly with Wilda after this."

"Just be yourself, honey. She likes you exactly as you are. You'd think you were her own the way she raves about your accomplishments."

Did he truly understand what they were dealing with, having a newshound living on the premises? "We were talking about Ryle, Dad."

"You were talking about Ryle. I dropped the subject five minutes ago." He started toward the hall, but stopped and looked over his shoulder at her. "Or maybe you aren't ready to let it go."

It was still dark when the toot of a car horn in the alley roused Dory from a restless sleep. Wondering who could be so inconsiderate, she propped on one elbow and widened the gap in the vertical blinds to see Harry's van parked under her window with headlights on and motor running.

Another toot, and Ryle loped down the steps between units 2 and 3, suitcases in hand, and satchel strapped around his shoulders.

Muttering under her breath, she snatched her kimono off the chair and slipped into it. Brushing her hair off her forehead with the heel of her hand, she threw the front door open. "Haggard," she called in a stage whisper. "Haggard."

"What are you doing up this time of night?" He wore a belted jacket that reminded her of a costume the leader of a safari might wear. "You wanted to see me off?"

"Three guesses."

"I woke you?" He smiled. Or did he? Expressions passed quickly over his mobile face. "I'm sorry."

"I was hoping I could persuade you to keep the racket down before you wake everybody in the court."

"I didn't realize how early it was," Harry said, too loud, passing by with more equipment on his way out to the van.

"Shhh."

He clapped a hand over his mouth and kept going.

"If the sun isn't up yet, you can assume the average person isn't either."

"Hey." Harry set down the bag. "I promised Meg I'd put up curtain rods in her bedroom. Would you tell her something came up and I'll be gone for a few days?"

Dory nodded. That was good news. It would give her a chance to deal with moving her trunks without someone breathing down her neck.

"Get that plaid case in the hall closet, will you?" Ryle slapped a hand to Harry's shoulder.

"Will do."

"I have executive portraits to do for Heckman and Heckman Associates in Flagstaff."

"Isn't that tame stuff for Mr. Intrepid?"

"Mr. Intrepid." His laugh was without mirth. "It's bread-and-butter stuff. Getting pictures of bigwigs for the company magazine. Something that makes them look human to their underlings."

"How do you manage that?"

"I squeeze off shots of them fly fishing, coaching little league, barbecuing for friends."

"Why does Harry go along?"

"He reminds people of their sons or their favorite nephews. He's invaluable at loosening people up."

"For the kill?"

"And he spells me on the driving." Ryle touched her face lightly and all sensation ran to the spot. "Go back to sleep, beauty."

She retied her sash for want of something to do with her hands. "I'll try."

"I enjoyed tonight." He thrust out his lower lip. "Or should I say last night?"

"Dad's a sensational cook."

His eyes caressed her face. "I wasn't talking about the stew."

Reliving the kiss that had left her completely lacking in resolve, Dory realized how she must look, with her hair in her face, her eyes full of sleep.

"I like the tousled look," he said, guessing the direction her thoughts were taking.

"Should I care?" she hurled back at him.

"Let's get the show on the road." Harry loomed up in time to preempt the chance of a good-bye kiss, if a kiss was Ryle's plan. "Don't forget to tell Meg, will you?"

"I won't," she promised. Not ready to let go of the moment, she stood in the darkness, with only a sliver of moon overhead, watching as the taillights of the van disappeared, nursing a sensation that was entirely new to her, not to mention unwelcome.

Chapter Four

It was after nine the next morning when Dory woke again, fixing her eyes on the pewter wind chime in the shape of an owl, which dangled in front of her closet.

Vaguely Dory remembered turning off her alarm and closing her eyes "for a few minutes." Ted had already left for the shop and had left a note addressed to "Sleepyhead."

Groggy, she poured herself a glass of orange juice. The toaster was set too high and her routine morning toast was too brown. She ate it anyway with Wilda's jam, then called the shop and told her father she was going to work at home again that day.

"Will you be here for lunch?" she asked, wondering if she should toss a salad.

"Wilda and I are going out for hot dogs. There's a

new place on Sycamore, she says, with sensational fixings.''

''Hot dogs?''

''Pure protein.''

''And fat.''

''Don't be a nag. I gotta go.''

The bracelet was the last of three she'd promised to deliver. Besides the gold and carnelian one she'd shown Ryle, she'd fashioned two others of silver— one with onyx stones and the other with turquoise. Though she'd strayed a bit from the original designs, she thought Lorraine would be pleased.

Though the work was important, at the moment something else took precedence. The trunk and foot-locker had to be moved while Ryle was gone. She was heading to the storage room when she remembered Harry and her promise about the curtain rods. Megan was working as receptionist for a software company in Scottsdale, but it was an afternoon job, and she might not have left yet.

''This assignment is nothing but phones, phones, and not a minute to myself.'' The girl's hair was smoothed into a sleek twist. Wearing a business suit and chunky heels, she looked entirely different from the usual Megan. ''To think I've got six more days of this.''

Following Megan to her stark white-and-black kitchen, Dory told her about the trip Harry was making with Ryle to Flagstaff. ''He didn't want you to think he'd forgotten the curtain rods.''

"Great." The girl carried her kettle to the sink and ran water in it. "I'll have no bedroom curtains for, what—three days? And I'm too drained at the moment to care. Would you like to have tea with me?"

"I can't."

"What's the point of being your own boss if you work like you're driven? Just don't forget Ryle's housewarming Saturday night."

The door seemed to tear away from its hinges and come to meet Dory head-on. "You didn't tell me about a housewarming."

"I didn't? Anyway, be sure to bring a present."

"I can't come. I have plans."

"It's obligatory. You know how I feel about such things, and I don't ask much." Megan sniffed the tea canister. "I wonder if this is still good."

"Megan, I can't come to your party."

"I thought the chip was off the shoulder. You invited Ryle to dinner last night. Harry saw him coming out of your place."

"It's a long story."

"Tell me later. But I fully expect to see you on Saturday, dressed to kill, and with an expectancy of having a fabulous time. Just remember: a Mr. America exterior is no guarantee a man's a bad guy."

"It's no guarantee he's a good one either," Dory countered.

She knew when she was beaten. Megan was being casual about her request, but she meant what she said. Her tenants were her family. That was why Dory had finally melted her reserve enough to trust Megan with secrets she'd never trusted to anyone else.

The leverage gained by keeping rent low allowed Megan to dictate terms of residence, and some were unusual.

"Dory," she called from the doorway. "Tell Ted to bring Wilda. The more the merrier. She'll bake one of her dreamy cream cakes, no doubt."

"Dad hates parties. I can't promise anything." Dory had no intention of mentioning the gathering to her father.

Maybe *she* was stuck with attending, but she hadn't spent the last fifteen years protecting her father, only to allow an inopportune housewarming to upset the apple cart. She'd drop in briefly, present Ryle with his gift, and that would be that.

Now she had to ram thoughts of Ryle to the dark crevices of her mind, and decide what to do about her store of memorabilia. Putting it off wasn't going to make it any easier.

The lid of the old trunk creaked as she opened it. The scent of another phase of her life tickled her nostrils, and she realized that, in spite of propaganda otherwise, passing time was a flop as a cure-all.

On top of everything was a yellow-and-white kitten quilt Dory and her mother had started together when Mrs. Brandt had been inspired by an article in a woman's magazine.

The tragedy at the hospital struck when they'd pieced only six out of twenty squares, and it had never been finished. Underneath was a dress her mother had made for Dory when she was nine. No seamstress, Mrs. Brandt. The hem had been uneven and the seams puckered.

A paisley-covered box held snapshots of her parents' courtship and honeymoon, as well as a scrapbook of formal shots of their wedding. Next came framed certificates Zachary Brandt had earned for his achievements in medicine, as well as awards bestowed for various contributions to the community.

More pictures of Zachary and his wife, Adele, dazzling and beautiful, both in evening attire. Newspaper clippings taken at a tennis club, and at the podium when Dr. Brandt had been asked to speak at one or another of his favorite charity functions.

Letters Zachary had written to Adele before they were married, and later, when he tried to persuade her to give their marriage another chance.

Unknown to her father, Dory had rescued everything and secreted it in the trunk, where it had remained.

At the bottom of the footlocker, under school papers and other childhood memorabilia, were clippings Dory had snipped from newspapers and magazines. Though they'd been cruel and hurtful, she'd been perversely fascinated by them. Steeling herself, she chose one and read it.

Under the photograph it said, *Pandora Brandt, 12, innocent victim of tragedy.*

Her child's eyes burned into her adult ones now as she remembered that day. Pressing her lips together, she put the piece on the floor beside her. Wasn't there a dolly somewhere in the trash area? Harry had used it when Megan bought a love seat at an estate sale in Mesa.

She found the dolly in the corner near the trash area.

Sturdy straps were provided to hold its burden steady, and she rolled it on creaky wheels over the threshold and down a series of shallow steps to bungalow one.

Finally succeeding in upending the trunk, she fastened it in place. Not until all was secure did she realize she'd neglected to put the newspaper clipping back. With a sigh, she stuck it in her pocket.

As she'd suspected, even with the footlocker standing on end, along with the trunk it took all the floor space in her closet. Her dresses couldn't hang full-length, and she had no choice but to line her shoes up on the lid. Seldom did her father find any reason to go in her room. Even then, as long as she kept the closet door closed, he wouldn't notice anything different.

Ted was home early, announcing that he and Wilda were going out to dinner. She was doing a write-up on a new Thai restaurant downtown, and the meal would be on the house.

"You're welcome to tag along," he told Dory.

"Thanks, but I have too much to do," she said truthfully. "I'll heat up the stew. It'll be even better the second day."

Once she was alone, though, she couldn't force herself back to her worktable. It was exactly as she'd feared when they'd first moved to Sherwood Forest. She needed to get the trunks out of the apartment, or she'd be tempted to go through them too often.

Drawn back to the bedroom, she found herself looking again at the old newspaper clipping.

The man who'd taken the picture had spotted her

trying to slip through the alley to a friend's house and had gallantly helped her make her escape, so the reporters in front of the building wouldn't see.

He'd bought her a grape Popsicle, and when he pointed his camera, she was too naive to realize what he planned.

"I didn't say that," she protested when she saw her picture in the paper, with the words the young man had twisted.

The quarrel that followed had brought an end to the Brandt marriage.

"This is too much," Adele Brandt raged. "Zach, you caused this by getting too close to your patients. I can't take it anymore."

That young photographer had been personable and earnest, exactly like Ryle. Dory had trusted him. Trust hadn't come easily to her since. She'd grown wiser in the last fifteen years.

Ryle and Harry returned Thursday morning, but they were so quiet about it this time, Dory didn't know they were back until she ran into Harry loading clothes in the dryer.

They'd had a successful trip, and finished ahead of schedule, he told her, bubbling with a desire to talk about the skill of his mentor. "Ryle's a master. I'm lucky to be working with him."

"I'll come back later," Dory said, trying to retreat gracefully.

"Stay. My stuff'll be dry before your washload goes through the rinse cycle." Harry punched the buttons that set the clothes in motion. "This one guy had a face like a bulldog, you know, and the last thing he wanted was to have his picture taken. So what we did was . . .''

''I see we have a full house.'' Ryle swung in with a laundry bag over his shoulder before Dory had a chance to break away. He wore a dark green shirt that made his tan look even richer.

''You two have priority,'' she managed, struggling against unreasoning joy at seeing him. ''When you've been on a trip, you always have plenty of laundry to do. Mine can wait.''

Ryle plopped his bag to the floor, and followed her outside. ''I tried to call you.''

''Why would you do that?'' She looked at him directly.

''To see if you were able to get back to sleep after we left.'' He spoke quietly, as if thrown off guard by her frosty tone.

''I did—eventually. By the way, I took my trunks out of your way. The storage room is all yours.''

When had she become so emotionally fragile? she wondered, quickening her pace in an effort to leave Ryle behind. Admittedly, this man was a challenge. Yes, as Harry had said, he was a master.

The zinnias in the planter outside the apartment were drooping reminders of her neglect. Not long ago she'd taken pleasure in the touch of perky color they brought.

''Sorry, little ones.'' She uncoiled the hose and yanked it over to give the flowers a refreshing drink. ''This won't happen again, I promise.''

They weren't all she'd neglected. Her work hadn't

been getting her full attention either. That would change from this moment on. No more would she allow Ryle Haggard to disrupt the order of her life.

"How do you decide what to get someone you don't know that well?" Wilda was saying, as Dory let herself in.

Dory's first thought was that the woman might as well move in, she'd been here so much lately. But even as she thought it, she felt petty. Hadn't she promised her father she'd make an effort to be friendly?

"Who are you talking about?" she asked lightly, taking her clothes basket to the service porch.

"Ryle, and the gift for the housewarming. What do you think about scented soap?" Wilda's voice was like the tinkle of glass bells.

"Don't ask me." How had the woman heard about the housewarming?

"Megan told me," Wilda said, reading the question in Dory's voice.

"I knew Dad wouldn't want to go," Dory explained. "He hates parties."

"Ted does need to socialize more."

Dory might have guessed Wilda was one of those men-are-little-boys-grown-tall types. In many ways she was downright officious. But she was so sweet about it, stepping on her wasn't easy.

Over the years a number of women had tried to push their way into Ted's life. He'd always managed to keep them at arm's length. This time he hadn't done very well.

"Ted thinks we should go with a paperweight,"

Wilda was saying. "The jasper stone Ryle admired so much."

When had Wilda and Ted become *we?* Dory didn't know what to say. "Dad put a lot of work into that globe."

"Exactly. It would make an exquisite gift."

"Have you seen my blue shirt?" Ted called from the other room.

"All your shirts are blue," Dory reminded him.

"The one with the stripe."

"It's still in the clothes basket. Unfortunately there's a queue in the laundry room."

Wilda made a clicking sound with her tongue. "Let me take your laundry home. I have my own washer-dryer combination."

Another attempt to make herself indispensable? "Don't bother. Dad can wear something else." Dory kept her tone nonchalant, but her father's uninterest in what he wore bothered her. She could remember when he never wore the same shirt twice without sending it to the laundry with precise instructions. "People will think that blue-striped shirt is a uniform."

"Ted's a man who likes to be comfortable," Wilda said. "And he always looks nice, don't you think? What did you buy for Ryle?"

"Nothing yet."

"Better hurry. The big night's almost here."

"I'll pick up something in Scottsdale tomorrow when I make my delivery."

It was one of those mild Arizona days when lemony sunlight made it difficult to stay indoors. The mountains were rust-colored against the cloudless sky. Birds chirped in celebration. The zinnias had perked up in appreciation of Dory's renewed attention, and she looked forward to her morning drive.

The car started with the turn of her key, as if it sensed she was thinking of replacing it. Her customer, a Scottsdale banker, was buying a necklace for his wife for their anniversary. Its links were set with assorted gemstones, adding up to the number of years they'd been married. Because it was to be a surprise, he didn't want Dory to bring it to the house. They met in the conference room of a hotel where he'd be having a meeting later in the day.

''Perfect.'' He turned the necklace so the rays of sun coming through the windows made the colors shimmer.

Dory had left the wrapping loose so the box could be opened. When he gave his approval, she did the final packaging, then showed him sketches for a bracelet they'd discussed for his mother's birthday.

''When can it be ready?''

She checked her appointment book and gave him a date.

As usual, she felt a special glow when a customer's appreciation was effusive. She stopped at a gift shop she'd passed earlier. Time to buy the housewarming gift.

A Native American man of about twenty-two showed her carvings. One, a kachina with fierce, bulging eyes and an open mouth filled with sharp teeth caught and held her attention. He had a feathered headdress and was carrying a spear.

"Carved out of cottonwood root. Not like some you buy, made of balsa."

"Mean-looking character, isn't he?"

"He's Chavejo, the enforcer. I can show you some that are more beautiful."

"This one's perfect," Dory decided, taking out her wallet. Let Ryle mull over the meaning behind the kachina's grotesque countenance.

In keeping with the Sherwood Forest theme, Dory wore a floor-length summer cotton dress for the housewarming. A print in blues and greens, its neckline was deep and square. The cut was straight to the hemline, only hinting at the narrowness of her waist.

Harry's assignment had been to lure Ryle away from the premises for the time it would take to prepare. In the nick of time, a news report about a hostage situation at a convenience store came over the radio, and armed with photographic paraphernalia, the two set off at breakneck speed.

"Some luck, huh?" Harry whispered, beaming, as he dashed in to tell Megan where they were going.

"Luck?" Dory marveled. "Doesn't he realize somebody could be killed?"

"When Harry was growing up his baby-sitter amused him with TV all day," Megan explained. "The good guy always caught the bad guy and everything turned out okay in the last ten minutes."

Dory shook her head. "So what's Ryle's excuse?"

Ryle, of the eyes that never lost their glint of humor, she thought morosely. Of the infectious smile and the practiced charm.

"Don't knock a man for the way he makes his living, kiddo," Megan retorted. "He's not one of the gunmen, after all."

While the news story had come at a convenient time, allowing Harry to get Ryle out from underfoot, it played havoc with Megan's timetable. After two hours had passed, and the guests were getting restless, she began to talk about setting the party for another night.

"And take down all that crepe paper?" Dory asked. Not to mention the pep talk she'd had to give herself to be there in the first place.

Megan shrugged. "What can I tell you?"

Fortunately Harry called a few minutes after nine to say that the culprits were in custody. "Get in position. We'll be back in a flash."

"Ask about the people at the convenience store," Dory said.

"Did everything come out okay?" Megan asked. She nodded as she listened. "Super. See you then."

"Well?"

"Harry says they got some great shots."

"I wasn't worried about their pictures." Dory groaned. "How about the hostages?"

"All fine. Okay. Look alive, Merry Men and Maids. Robin Hood will be here in twenty minutes."

Chapter Five

Grace Ann, the nurse in unit 1, had done the decorations, all greens and browns, like a genuine forest. Megan's job was to keep hot food hot, and cold food cold. Though she'd specified that everyone do the best they could, wearing clothes in keeping with the period, her own dress was slit to the knee.

"Not exactly Maid Marian," she admitted. "But maybe the original Marian would have ended up with Robin if she'd worn something like this."

Slightly disheveled, probably from stampeding competing photojournalists, Ryle acted properly surprised when he unlocked the front door to find his apartment full of people.

"Et tu, Brute?" he muttered out of the corner of his mouth as he passed Dory.

She smiled sweetly. "I would have thought being guest of honor would be right up your alley."

"You would have thought wrong."

His apartment was a hodgepodge that reflected his personality. A well-worn couch in a tweedy fabric. An old windup record player, used for storage. An atrocious clock with the man in the moon in its middle, a line of old-time cast-iron toys on a ledge over the windows.

While he was in a daze, he was led to the couch and presents were piled in front of him. Grace Ann had brought a doorstop in the shape of a dachshund. Megan's gift was an antique fountain pen. Harry's was a desk planner. Dory had second thoughts about her present as she watched him tear off the silver paper.

"It's Chavejo," she explained when he stared at it.

"Ugly little critter," Harry cracked, shivering.

"If it weren't ugly it wouldn't be able to scare anybody into behaving himself," Grace Ann's escort said. He was a tall man with a pencil-thin mustache, reminiscent of the Thin Man of film fame.

"Is that what it's supposed to do?" Ryle shifted his glance to Dory.

"It's the Hopi version of the see-no-evil, hear-no-evil monkeys," the Thin Man went on.

"Except Ryle would be out of business if he saw no evil, wouldn't he?" Dory asked, enjoying herself at his expense.

"He's a kind of enforcer," the man said, echoing what the youth in the shop had told Dory earlier. "My nephew's collected a number of these. Some are for children. This fellow's designed to keep adults in line.''

"It's a doll?'' Megan grimaced.

"You don't play with it. You hang it somewhere it can be safe.''

"Or where you can be safe from it.'' Ryle held it at arm's length. "Thanks, Dory—I think.''

"Don't drop this.'' Wilda handed Ryle the beautifully polished jasper.

"It's a beauty.'' Ryle looked genuinely pleased.

"You can never have too many paperweights,'' Wilda said brightly.

"Is everybody ready to eat?'' Megan hit the edge of a knife several times against a glass. "Grab a plate.''

There were no entrées, just appetizers of all kinds; canapes and dips, sliced meats, and cheeses with bacon and chives, all bought from the special section of a market, ready-prepared. Everything was delicious, and there was four times as much as they would have needed for the number of people attending the party.

Wilda and Grace Ann were arguing the pros and cons of patchwork and appliquéd quilts. The Thin Man and Ted were discussing the history of the paperweight, and Ryle was caught up in a conversation with Megan.

Dory, who'd been wandering around the apartment, thinking about the man who'd furnished it, ventured down a short hallway. To one side stood an oak cabinet with double glass doors and a slot for a skeleton key. Inside was a collection of vintage cameras. On top lay a stack of eight-by-ten photographs. Out of the corner of her eye she noticed that Ryle had followed her.

"Yours?" She studied a picture taken at the finish line of a horse race. Though there were spectators in the shot too, the background was a blur, accentuating the feeling of movement.

He nodded.

The animals, one black and one chestnut, were sleek and beautiful. "At least you didn't invade anyone's privacy to get the shot," she said.

"Ever been to the racetrack?"

"No." She turned to the next picture, taken at the winner's circle, then turned back to the original. "These horses are racing with every inch of their being. You'd think they cared about the outcome."

"They do."

"The winner gets an extra sugar cube?"

"They sense the exhilaration of their owners and their riders."

She made no other comment as she moved to the next photo. The subject was a child who'd been terrified by a fireworks display. The genuine fear had been captured, as well as the mother's gentleness as she tried to quiet the little girl. This was more like the Ryle Dory knew and resented.

The brown of his eyes looked rich in the dim light of the hall. He was still wearing the peaked hat Megan had plunked on his head, and he actually looked like Robin Hood. She could imagine him swinging out of the trees, executing a deep bow, and saying, "Welcome to Sherwood Forest, milady"

"Isn't there a law against blinding unsuspecting

people with your flashbulbs?'' Dory asked, disturbed. ''Without asking if it's okay?''

''A bystander at a public function is fair game.''

A chill zigzagged to the nape of her neck. As she and her father had been fair game those long years ago? ''It comes under the public's right to know?''

He nodded.

''If it weren't for that little technicality and those who take advantage of it, supermarket rags would be out of business, wouldn't they?''

His smile came and went more quickly than usual. ''You never read checkout-line literature?''

''How can anyone not read it? It looms in front of us, screaming new lies.''

''But you don't buy the magazines?''

''As a matter of fact, I have a collection of the more outrageous stories. My favorite is a headline proclaiming that Sherlock Holmes is alive, and working as a private detective in Minneapolis.''

''So while detecting, he stumbled across the secret to eternal youth?''

''No one is hurt by that story. It's too ridiculous to be taken seriously. It's the others I have a quarrel with.'' She looked at the next picture. It had been taken at a hospital, where a rock singer was fighting off the press as he tried to gain entrance. ''This one is an invasion of privacy.''

''I suppose you think Mathew Brady shouldn't have been allowed to photograph the Civil War battlefields.''

If he saw himself as a modern-day Mathew Brady

he was even more egotistical than she'd imagined. "He was a historian. Not a . . . a headline seeker."

Her comment didn't sit well with Ryle. "The food is great," he said tightly, new darkness swirling in his eyes. "I think I'll go back for seconds. Excuse me."

He didn't seek her out anymore that night. In fact, he made a point to involve himself in conversation with the others. A game Megan had devised, like charades, but with a Sherwood Forest theme, took up the rest of the evening. Players had to remember which actor played which role in the movie to win dinner for two at Megan's favorite French restaurant, Robaire's. Grace Ann's escort, who won, was the first to say good night. The others followed soon after.

Ryle's hand pressed Dory's fingers as he mouthed a thank-you when she prepared to leave. But his gaze was as hard as petrified wood, informing her that she wouldn't have to worry about his advances anymore.

She was emotionally exhausted, she reminded herself. That was why having succeeded in alienating him didn't bring her the sense of relief she'd expected it would.

Later, when she came out of the bathroom after a perfumed soak, she found Ted in his favorite chair, reading, though she'd supposed he was in bed. Wilda had bought him a book of poetry when she picked up the wrapping paper for Ryle's present. Walt Whitman.

"This guy makes sense," he said, noticing Dory beside him.

She had to smile. Ted wasn't usually a fan of poetry. She bent to kiss the top of his head where his scalp showed through.

"No problems tonight, were there?" He smiled up at her. "So forget the past and look forward to the rest of your life."

"Can you forget?"

He hesitated for a moment, and then looked serious. "If you'll let me."

She swallowed an ache in her throat. As if he could ever forget having to give up his profession, and the reputation he worked so long and so hard to achieve. "I'm going to bed now."

Dory had loved Sherwood Forest at first sight, sensing after she'd met and spoken with Megan—funny and serious at the same time—that she and her father had found a home.

She'd furnished her room for keeps—a bit at a time, painting walls and alcoves a soft peach, dressing the light oak floors with a gray shag rug she'd had a difficult time finding, since shag was out of fashion. Then there was the Marc Chagall poster she'd adored on sight, with its bold colors and childlike images. The brass bed she'd found in a secondhand shop, and spread lovingly with her paternal grandmother's handmade quilt with its peach and gray swirls.

As she absently brushed her hair, she pondered what her father had said. Were they old news? She wasn't so sure.

Writers were always coming up with new tidbits about Abraham Lincoln, Marilyn Monroe, George Armstrong Custer. The public never tired of reading about them. Doctors had their own brand of celebrity.

Especially handsome, successful ones like Zachary Brandt. A new angle would be welcomed by people as far as newspapers reached.

She stared at her mirror image, mentally going over her conversation with Ryle at the party. Had she antagonized him so much that he'd sniff a story out, and succeed in discovering that angle?

She still hadn't shaken her worry free the next day, on her way to the shop. As she signaled for a left turn into the driveway, she almost lost her footing on the bike pedal. The man who'd come to the apartment, hurling threats and shouting, was across the street buying a newspaper from the rack.

"Dad!" The bell over the door jangled as she ducked inside.

A whirring sounded at the rear of the shop, and Ted called, "Back here, honey."

"I saw Harvey Ott outside." She dropped her handbag on the counter, and scurried toward her father's voice. A surge of electricity passed from her eyebrows to her toes when she saw that he wasn't alone.

Ryle was at his elbow, watching him work. Evidently his resentment of Dory didn't stretch to include her father.

Ted clicked off the machine. "Ott owns a metal and trim shop down a couple of blocks, on Fairbrook."

"You don't think he's stalking you?" She returned Ryle's nod of acknowledgment with one of her own. He was as dashing as usual, unfortunately, in a white shirt, open at the collar, and loose-fitting gray slacks.

"I'm sure we're safe." Ted removed his protective

glasses. ''Aren't you supposed to be on your way to Kingman?''

''I was afraid to trust the car for a long drive.'' Dory didn't like to be late on a promised delivery, especially to Lorraine Frye, but it couldn't be helped.

''When are you gonna get rid of that clunker? It's more trouble than it's worth.''

''I'm keeping an eye open for a good deal. Meanwhile, I biked here, hoping I could borrow the truck.''

''Sorry. I have a meeting uptown this afternoon, and I don't see myself biking.''

''How about a city bus?''

''Loaded down with samples?'' Ted chuckled.

''I meant to head over Kingman way soon.'' Ryle crooked an elbow to look at his watch. ''If you don't mind a side trip, I'll give you a lift.''

Shouldn't he have been off somewhere running down scandals? Or did he sense one in his own backyard?

''I need shots of Justice, a ghost town about half an hour off the main highway,'' he elaborated. ''It's the real thing. Not one of these commercialized settings with picture postcards for sale, refreshment stands, and motels.''

''I know about Justice.'' Her father had organized several digs near the long-decayed town. ''I wouldn't think there'd be anything in weathered boards to excite you.''

''You'd be surprised at what excites me.''

''Thanks, but it wouldn't work,'' she said briskly. ''There wouldn't be enough time for both errands.''

He didn't comment, but bent to study a tray of cuff

links Ted had put in the display case that morning, as if he couldn't care less about being turned down.

"Maybe I could rearrange my meeting." Ted wiped his fingers on a handy cloth. "Let me make a few calls."

"Wait." The moment Dory refused, she regretted it. Not only did she need the ride, but it might serve a useful purpose. If she oozed friendliness during the long drive, she might succeed in getting him off her father's trail. "I'll take you up on your offer, Ryle, if you let me pay for the gas."

Ted chuckled at Ryle's grimace. "Don't fight her, son. At least let her buy lunch. She's a determined one."

"I would never have guessed," Ryle said wryly.

"Are you sure it won't be too much trouble?" Dory asked, almost hoping he'd back out.

"If it was too much trouble, I wouldn't have suggested it." The tight quirk of his lips assured her that he hadn't forgotten her comments at the party. All wasn't peaches and honey between them.

"I'll only be a minute." She yanked aside the curtains that blocked off the section of the shop where she and her father kept a few items of clothing for emergencies.

Often as Ted worked, he spattered mud on his shirt or pants and had to change. Dory liked to present a professional image too, when she made a delivery. The ankle-length summer cotton in a navy-and-white print would fit the image of artisan more than the knee-length shorts she'd worn for her trip here on her bike, she decided. Lorraine Frye expected a designer of whatever jewelry she commissioned to dress like a designer of jewelry.

Ryle hooted in disapproval when he saw her outfit. "Shorts would have been more practical for the desert."

"I'll be on business first, remember?" she asked, not about to let him dictate what she wore.

Traffic was easygoing once they left the heart of town and passed through outlying communities of family motels, Laundromats, and kids skating off wooden ramps built in the dirt.

"I wouldn't think you'd find an outlet for your work in Kingman," he said when they'd reached the open highway. "Tourists get out to stretch their legs there and buy souvenirs. They're not looking for anything unique or costly."

"Actually my customer owns a souvenir shop. She lives in Kingman because the desert gives her a welcome respite from stop-and-go living. But she has more elegant stores all along the West Coast."

"How did you two find each other?"

"Dad and I met her at a gem show three years ago. She bought a pendant I'd designed, and ordered a couple of other pieces. Since then she's been in touch with me off and on for customers who wanted something made to their own specifications."

"So it's worth the trip to make the delivery?"

"Over and over again, even if I didn't enjoy the drive."

"It doesn't get old?"

"Never. I especially like it in the spring, when the Joshua trees are in bloom, and the lupine and phlox have a perfect backdrop of wide blue sky.'' She gazed at the passing scenery as if enjoying it for the first time. ''Have you noticed that the rock formations change, depending on the angle of the sun?''

''You've sold me.''

That, she hadn't meant to do. ''I imagine spring is beautiful everywhere.''

''Ever been out of the state?''

''A time or two.'' Nervous, she moistened her lower lip with her tongue.

''You attended the University of Arizona?''

''Yes,'' she answered after a moment's contemplation, deciding he wasn't curious enough at this point to investigate records and discover that it wasn't true—that she'd finished school in New Mexico. ''What about you? What made you decide to take up photography?''

Growing accustomed to Dory's rash changes of subject, Ryle didn't flinch. ''When I was in the sixth grade, I did a science project, taking photographs with a camera I'd made from a shoebox. From that point on I read every book I could get on the subject.

''When I was old enough, I got a job in a catalog house. Not much art involved. I sold a few pictures to newspapers while I was in college, then got hired as an assistant to a successful freelancer.''

''The way Harry's doing?''

''You can learn only so much in a classroom.''

''That's true in jewelry making too.''

He reached toward the radio. ''Would you like some music?''

''Fine,'' she said amiably.

The cassette he set in motion with a jab of his index finger was soothing—instrumental, with strings and piano. "What spiked your interest in fashioning jewelry?" he asked, turning the volume low.

"My father and his interest in gemstones. It followed naturally. Was this freelancer you worked for stationed in Chicago?"

He narrowed one eye, studying her briefly, before he answered. "Atlanta. I worked like a demon to make myself indispensable, and it ended with him taking me on assignments to London and Paris. Most of this was the fashion industry, which, contrary to what you might suppose, was fast moving and exciting."

Every time he asked a question, Dory shot one back at him. For a while they played a verbal tennis game. Then he began relating stories about his early experiences. About his youthful overconfidence that lost him an interview with a reluctant recluse. About another time when he went to cover a gala Broadway opening, so excited about the assignment he forgot to put film in his camera.

Last week he'd done an assignment on day-care centers. "I enjoyed it," he admitted. "But with some of those kids, what with throwing sand and aiming metal shovels at my shins, it was like being in the trenches."

"This was one of those situations where Harry came in handy, I'll bet."

"He would have, if he'd been available. But he has a heavy load of classes this semester."

Harry, at twenty-three, had only recently started college. Though he would rather have jumped right into a career in photography, his uncle, who was sending supplementary checks until he was self-supporting, insisted he get the diploma Harry referred to as a "useless piece of paper." Meanwhile, he did jobs for Ryle to allow him to buy extras.

As the miles flew past the car window, Dory felt layers of self-consciousness peel away. Enjoying his company in spite of herself, she discovered that they'd arrived at their destination sooner than she'd expected they would.

Likely hoping for a disaster to photograph, Ryle meandered down one side of the street and back again, looking in windows, while she ducked into the Vanishing American with her case.

Lorraine had a frantic hairdo of gray curls, and eyebrows penciled into perpetual astonishment. Her wraparound skirt was hand-painted in Southwestern colors, and enamel earrings echoing those colors dangled from her ears. She oohed and aahed over Dory's work. "I can't tell you how many favorable comments I've had on my ring." She wriggled her fingers to display one of the purchases she'd made on Dory's last visit— a unicorn with amethyst eyes.

"I thought you were putting it on sale."

"I decided to keep it for myself."

As they sipped coffee, Lorraine approved sketches Dory presented for a necklace design. "Will you be at the gem show this year?" she asked Dory.

"We don't like to close the shop on a weekend. It's our busiest time."

"Couldn't you hire a temporary counter person to watch for you?"

"I doubt it. Lots of our customers come in for advice and to sit around and trade stories with my father. I can't give them much technical information, but I can lend an interested ear."

"Oh, my. What's this?" Distracted, the woman donned the glasses she wore on a velvet ribbon around her neck and rose, looking toward the street. "Is that impressive hunk of masculinity with you?"

Ryle had returned to the car and was leaning against it, squinting into the sun as he waited. Looking at him through the eyes of a stranger, who didn't know his relentless drive for recognition, Dory had to admit he presented an appealing picture.

"He's a tenant in our apartment complex. My car wouldn't start, and he offered to drive me here."

"Ah, yes. The old car-won't-start routine."

"It wouldn't," Dory insisted.

"Next time don't be so selfish. Bring your hero inside."

Chapter Six

After roast-beef sandwiches and iced tea at a nearby café, Ryle bought a wide-brimmed straw hat. Without saying anything, he plunked it on Dory's head, pausing to tuck in a strand of satiny hair. "You'll blister without it."

"I have hats at home," she objected, distracted by the daisy that bobbed from its brim.

"A lot of good they're doing there."

He was right. But when she'd left the apartment she hadn't counted on the trek to Justice. "I'll reimburse you."

He held up one hand. "You already embarrassed me by fighting over the lunch check."

"We had a deal. I was to pay for lunch, remember?"

78

"A deal I didn't make. But okay. Can we leave it at that?"

"I suppose so," she agreed, and they were off on his errand. Perversely, considering her wariness, she had to admit she looked forward to it.

Arizona, like other states in the Southwest, was peppered with ghost towns, grim reminders of mines that had played out, crushing dreams. The terrain was seamed with canyons and steep ledges where boulders barely perched, as if ready to tumble at the slightest provocation. Sagebrush and weedy grasses choked the dry gullies, adding to the appearance of inhospitality.

A victim of weather and overgrowth, Justice would have been easy for a visitor to miss, if he didn't know exactly where to look. No other cars were in sight as they took the decided rise.

After parking in a patch of shade from a stunted cottonwood, Ryle pulled two cans of root beer from an ice chest, popped the tops, and handed Dory one. "You'll be cooler if you get out of the car. There could be a breeze."

She peered into the hazy heat. "A breeze?"

He shrugged. "A couple of vultures might fly over, flapping their wings."

Noting that the air inside the car was getting thicker by the minute, she accepted his hand getting out.

"You'll need something to sit on while I'm working." He pulled an Army blanket out of the trunk.

"I don't need that."

"Maybe you wouldn't, if you'd worn something

knockabout.'' He raised an eyebrow. ''On second thought, I'm glad you're wearing the dress. It has a vintage look that'll inspire me.''

''I didn't think photographers needed inspiration.''

''Everybody needs inspiration.''

''Even plumbers?'' she teased, remembering his father's ambitions for him.

His laugh was a snort. ''Plumbers more than most.''

Tucking the blanket under his arm, he gripped her elbow, and together they climbed toward what had once been the main street. Before long, the years would erase all signs of civilization. The weathered structures that remained didn't have roofs or even full sets of walls.

''Why would anyone build on such a hilly site?'' she asked.

''Gold is where you find it.''

Undaunted by the upward trek, he left Dory sitting on the blanket in a square of semishade offered by a broken wagon, and crouched, knelt, and lunged over rotted limbs and weathered rails, trying for angles he wanted. A few times he even flopped on his stomach to snap pictures of hanging doors, broken windows, and rusty bedsprings.

When his feats began, Dory found it impossible to wrench her gaze away. He was not only Robin Hood; he was Indiana Jones and Tarzan. Being with him made her feel she was part of a venture into the past.

After he'd given a fat, reddish brown bug more attention than it warranted, he helped her to her feet and they climbed together toward a cave, where over a half century before someone had carved initials in the rock, inspiring another set of pictures.

Some shots looked to Dory exactly like others he'd taken a few minutes before, but he seemed to have stepped into another dimension as he snapped, snapped, and snapped again. She wasn't bored. Watching him was far too intriguing.

"What's wrong?" he asked, aware of her scrutiny.

You're what's wrong, the other, more outspoken Dory inside her dared her to say. *You, Ryle Haggard. Today, right now, you're everything a woman could ever hope for in a man.*

"It's so sad here," she whispered, hoping her answer would keep him from guessing all she was feeling.

Looking solemn, he touched a finger to a place under her chin, bringing back the memory of his kiss. Would she ever experience it again? "I wouldn't want to spoil your day. Let's go back."

When they'd picked their way down to the main street again, Dory paused at a crumbling cabin, where a gangly yellow blossom struggled through the cracked earth. "Someone once planted seeds that were great great-grandparents of this little waif," she said softly, "trying to make the land more homelike."

"Some of these camps developed into real communities with post offices and schools. Mineral Park even had a newspaper."

"Did anyone ever find what they were looking for?"

"More than thirty million in ore was taken out of the Cerbats at the turn of the century."

''And then the veins played out.'' She moved a hand gingerly up and down the post that supported the porch.

''Watch for splinters,'' he cautioned.

She pulled back. ''Imagine. A young couple building a house here. The man baking in the sun all day. The woman trying in vain to sweep out sand and dirt. All for nothing.''

''Maybe the folks in this particular cabin moved on when they made their fortune.''

''I don't think so.''

Discovery and loss, she thought. Was anything more heart-wrenching?

His eyes glittered as he studied her, his skin faintly glowing from the heat. His arms around her would be like chains. Never had she felt so compelled to comb her fingers through the tangle of a man's sun-touched hair, to hug him close and feel his heart pound.

Or was she capable of making Ryle's heart pound? Had there been too many women in his life—glamorous, exciting women—to allow him to get excited by one woman's kiss?

''Are you about to cry?'' Ryle asked, wondering about the mistiness in her eyes.

''Don't mind me.'' She tried for a smile. ''I cry over Lassie movies.''

''So do I.''

When silence fell between them, it was different from any silence Dory had ever known. It didn't beg to be filled with empty conversation. It was bonding and comfortable.

Unfortunately, there was another part to this man—

a part that could cold-bloodedly weigh the pain of a tragedy's victim against its dollar value. This was a part she could never accept.

Discovery and loss.

Now was the perfect moment for him to gather her in his arms and trade kiss for kiss. She almost thought he would. Instead he began walking again. "Enough dallying. There's work to be done."

"So get to it," she shot back, bristling at his use of the word *dallying*.

"Would you mind posing for me?"

The question brought up her feelings of self-consciousness, and she couldn't believe he'd asked it. "I sure would."

"You sure would pose, or sure would mind?"

She cleared her throat, hoping to make her voice firm. "I refuse to honor that ridiculous question with an answer, Mr. Haggard."

"You aren't on the ten-most-wanted lists, are you, by chance? Afraid of being spotted by John Law?" When she didn't answer, he took another swig of his root beer, though it would be unappetizingly warm now. "Then how about my taking a picture of your shadow?"

"Where's the shock value in a shadow?"

He made a fist and held it under her nose. "Can we do this without the wisecracks? You owe me. I gave up a whole day to drive you to Kingman."

"You—you gave up . . ." she sputtered. "By way of a thank-you-sir, I treated you to an excellent roast-beef sandwich. Not to mention an iced tea, with refills."

''I bought you that stylish straw hat to pay for the sandwich.''

''A hat I didn't want.''

''A hat you've been using to protect the end of your pretty nose from sunburn.''

''Sunburn caused by your desert sun.''

''*My* desert sun?''

She laughed, and he laughed too, at their manufactured argument. ''Very well.''

''What's that mean—very well? I don't think I've ever heard anyone actually say that.''

''You may photograph my shadow. Only my shadow. If I see the business end of that camera aimed in my direction, I won't be responsible for what I throw at you.''

The air was thick. Dust burned Dory's feet through the soles of her shoes. Ever mindful of the camera lens, she allowed herself to be posed next to a wagon wheel, the remains of an old well, and beside a rusting farm implement.

While he fussed with his camera, changing f-stops, or whatever he needed to do to make his photography work, Dory shook damp hair away from the back of her neck and started up the steps of one of the cabins for an exploration of her own.

''Watch those boards.'' He dropped the blanket on the edge of the porch. ''They're rotted through.''

''I'm watching.''

Bouncing a few times, he tried his weight on the rough planks inside, where the spaces had widened so much she could see the ground beneath them. ''Keep to the outside wall.''

The cabin was only one room. Half a table, and a chair with three legs sat crookedly in the middle of the floor. In a crude alcove was a cot. Under it lay a faceless doll made from a burlap sack.

Dory started to pick it up, then changed her mind. "Are we finished here?" Experiencing another wave of unreasoning sadness, she backed toward the door.

"Watch it," Ryle cautioned again. "Follow me. Step where I step."

As he moved onto the porch, a board sank under his weight. But this time instead of springing back, it gave way, too quickly for him to jump to steady ground. He reached for the rail, but it gave too, pulling with it what was left of the porch roof. Flailing his arms, he landed with a thud on the other side, where he slid down the gravelly incline with a surprised outcry.

Dory, who'd been ahead of him, scooped up the blanket and camera and leaped clear just in time. She scurried over to the slope, fearful of what she might find. "Are you—are you all right?"

His answer was a growl.

Dropping to one knee, she offered a hand, but as he tried to grab it he slid farther, then farther, until his progress was stopped by the exposed roots of a gnarled sycamore.

"Excuse me if I don't step where you step," she called down when, apparently unhurt, he sat muttering to himself.

"Got the camera?" he asked.

"The camera's fine. Which button do I push?" Teasing, she swung it into position.

"I don't want you to take my picture; I want . . ." He groaned and lay back again. "Come down here. I need you."

After setting the camera safely to one side, away from possible falling debris, she returned to the slope, where Ryle wasn't even trying to get up. "Is anything broken?" Maybe he was only being macho, not wanting to tell her he was in pain.

When he didn't reply she started down, planting her feet carefully in the crumbling earth, trying her position each time. As she neared the place where he lay, he clamped his fingers around her wrist and yanked, causing her to slide the last two feet, and to land beside him with a thud.

"Look at what you did to my dress," she sputtered.

"Never mind. I'll wash it for you when we get back."

"You'll wash it? I can see that."

He tried to look insulted. "I'm very good at laundry. I've been doing it since I was sixteen. Relax."

"Relax, here? With sharp rocks and thorns under me? Your face is bleeding." Gingerly she brought a finger to within a half inch of an angry scratch. "You need to put something on it. Don't you carry first-aid equipment?"

"I have a snakebite kit."

"You weren't bitten by a snake."

"The day is young." Steadying himself with a toe against the tree root, he stretched until he caught the edge of the blanket Dory had dropped when she slid. Rolling over to one side, he smoothed it on the ground. "Put this under you. You'll be more comfortable."

"I don't want to be comfortable."

He grinned. "You know, sometimes I believe that. But I can't kiss a girl who isn't comfortable."

His mere pronouncing of the word *kiss* made her suck in her breath involuntarily. "Who said anything about kissing?"

"No need. We've been leading up to it since we met."

"I didn't know we were leading up to anything."

"Sure you do. It's why you bared your claws."

"Is that what you finally decided?" Her lips were so dry she could hardly get her words past them.

"Afraid?"

"Hardly." She tried to laugh.

"Then." He waited.

"Fine," she agreed blithely. Meaning to demonstrate that she wasn't at all fearful of falling under his spell, she leaned over and planted a perfunctory kiss at one corner of his mouth, then the other. "There."

"There?" he questioned.

It was no use. The contact had felt too good for comfort. Determined to escape the sphere of his influence, she rolled to her feet and scrambled up the slope before he could realize what she planned.

"Hey. Can't a man have a few minutes to recuperate from his injuries?"

"You've had long enough," she sang out with more lightness than she felt. "We want to get home before dark."

"Why?" Grumbling under his breath, he followed her, and in moments they were on their way, with the blanket under his arm and his camera strapped over his shoulder. As they neared the car, Dory stopped for a final look.

"Something wrong?" Ryle asked.

Yes. Everything was wrong. The two of them, together like this, meant even more trouble than she realized. "I—I was thinking of the people who lived in the cabin."

"Our starry-eyed young couple again?" He shook his head. "For all you know it was two or three grizzled old miners who threw in together, hoping to make their fortune."

"It wasn't." Her gaze rested on the fork of the old oak tree, where a deep slash in the bark had healed. "The husband would return to the cabin at night, too tired from swinging his pickax to do more than wolf down rations meant for only a few days, which his poor wife had to stretch to last a few weeks."

A smile quivered on Ryle's lips. "You can't know all that."

"Yes, I can." From somewhere Dory heard the squawk of a nameless bird. Thinking of the faceless doll in the dust, she lowered her eyes and reached for the door handle. "There was a child."

"You're a puzzle, Dory Brandt," he said, a curious look replacing his smile after he'd tucked her inside the car. "A real puzzle."

"You should talk," she countered.

Though she expected him to climb in too, he didn't. He only stood, staring back the way they had come, as if he spied something he'd missed before. "Hold on a minute."

''What is it?'' All she could see was a rusty tin can under a ruined rail fence.

Uttering a token moan of impatience, she waited while he trotted over, circled his subject, lay flat on his stomach, and pressed off a few shots.

''It's a long ride home, Haggard,'' she called, chagrined that he could so easily find his way back to the world of clicking shutters after the closeness they'd shared a moment before.

''I'm coming.''

''You needed pictures of a tin can?'' she wanted to know, when they were finally on their way.

''It said something to me.''

''It said something to you,'' she repeated, looking out the window at the line of scraggly pines that zoomed past.

''Would you like to see me in action sometime?'' he asked, when pine had again given way to tumbleweed and saguaro.

Her lips still tingled from touching his. ''I've already seen you in action.''

He grinned. ''I meant—maybe you'd like to watch me develop what we took today. Want to investigate the mysteries of the darkroom?''

She'd investigated enough mysteries today to think about anymore. ''Sometime.''

''Said the fly to the spider.''

''No, I would. Sometime.''

He nodded, not believing her. ''Sometime seems to be a safe distance in the future.''

''Maybe,'' she admitted, part of her still climbing

the dusty hill, with Ryle's hand holding hers. Part of her always would be.

"Except that I won't leave it at that. I'll remind you," he said.

As if she needed reminding.

Chapter Seven

Megan lifted her glass of cola in a toast as Dory and Ryle straggled toward her. Harry, wearing a baseball cap backward, was working at the laptop.

"Ambitious today?" Dory asked breezily, wanting to make up for the frosty way she'd treated him lately because of his connection with Ryle.

He didn't look up. "I'm working on a new filing system. Ryle's system eludes me."

"It eludes me too." Ryle swung his shoulder bag to the deck and stretched.

"Where have you two been?" Megan shaded her eyes with one hand.

"My car wasn't up to a long drive, so Ryle offered to take me to Kingman," Dory explained.

"A nice, smooth ride in an air-conditioned car? Why so bedraggled?"

"You're sitting under an umbrella," Dory reminded her. "The sun is merciless in the desert."

"I thought your delivery was in town."

"Ryle needed pictures of a ghost town."

"You're kidding!" Harry slid a proof sheet into a waiting envelope before turning in his chair to face them. "We've already got hundreds. Jerome, Cerbat, and Mineral Park, to name a minuscule few." His face changed as he caught his friend's expression, and he realized he'd said the wrong thing. "Uh—that is, we can always use a few more. With uh—different shadow patterns and such."

"Shadow patterns do make a difference, don't they?" Megan teased, not missing the signal that moved back and forth between the two men.

Dory hadn't missed it either. So Ryle had only invented a reason for making the drive. Was he simply being helpful, or did he have a more devious motive?

"Hey, Meg." Harry's voice was too hearty as he initiated a change of subject. "Tell these people about your book getting published."

"You found a publisher?" It was difficult to envision. Megan's rhymes were laughably forced, and her subjects trite.

"Harry thinks the way to go is self-publishing." Megan leaned forward. "So I can call the shots. Make decisions without seeing my favorite lines blue-penciled."

Ryle snorted. "You'll end up with a garage full of books. And a flattened bank account."

"Harry has a friend who'll set everything up for an absolute minimum." Megan clasped her hands behind her head. "What a thrill it'll be. I've been writing since I was thirteen, with absolutely no success. It's impossible these days for an unknown to have her talents recognized."

"If seeing your work in print is the whole point, go for it." Ryle sat heavily on the rail. "As long as you don't count on getting your money back."

Megan pouted. "Anything is possible."

"Anything but teaching an elephant to fly, and making money out of self-publishing a book of poetry."

"Does everything have to be about money?" Dory couldn't help asking, reminded unpleasantly of the out-for-fame-and-fortune side of Ryle's nature. "What about personal satisfaction?"

"Depends on how much you're prepared to lose."

"I remember hearing that Rod McKuen financed the printing of his first book." Harry squinted at the computer screen. "It worked for him."

"McKuen played the lecture circuit," Ryle reminded them. "His audience bought the books directly."

"I'm not averse to lecturing." Megan examined her fingernails. "I'm an expert at reading with drama and pathos."

"That you are, babe," Harry agreed. "You can make a grown man cry."

"It's a ten-million-to-one shot," Ryle said. "Unless a poet already has a reputation."

"Reputation." Irritated by the damper he was putting on her friend's joy, Dory fluttered one hand. "Maybe if she held up a bank, it would make her famous enough."

''That'd do it,'' Ryle agreed. ''The Poet Bandit. Books signed on visitors' day at the county lockup.''

''Robbery is out.'' Megan hooted. ''I might get shot trying to escape.''

Harry laughed. ''Even better. Dying makes people popular.''

''I believe I'll try another way to get famous, if you don't mind.''

''You could threaten to jump off a building,'' he offered.

''Be sure and tell Ryle in advance,'' Dory said through clenched teeth. ''He'll want to take pictures.''

Less than pleased with her about-face, Ryle arrowed a scowl at Dory, and snatched up his bag. ''I have to go.''

''You can say that again.'' Harry checked his watch. ''They were expecting you at the Koenig Gallery an hour ago.''

''Ouch.'' Ryle slapped a hand to his head. ''Maybe I'll skip it tonight.''

''You're kidding, aren't you? It's bad enough you won't be on hand to turn cartwheels for your public for the rest of the week.''

''I know. I know.''

Megan shook her head. ''I assumed that photographers lived and breathed for the moment they had these showings.''

''They do,'' Ryle admitted. ''But I'm on the road again early in the morning.''

''Where to this time?''

''Brochures for a renovated hotel in Santa Fe.'' As

Ryle started away, he looked back at Dory. "Would you, by chance, like to ride along?"

A truthful answer to his question would have been a resounding yes. But it wouldn't have been a wise one, considering how vulnerable she was where he was concerned. "To carry your bags?"

"Might as well put you to work." Ryle flashed his on-again, off-again grin. "It's a town people fall in love with on sight. Ever been there?"

Dory swallowed, not wanting to be pushed into a lie. She and her father had lived in Santa Fe for three years. Ted hadn't owned his own business then, but had worked at a store that sold clothing and leather goods.

A movie director, filming in Taos, visited the shop, recognized Zachary Brandt, and called his presence to the attention of the press.

While the story in the papers had been short-lived, friends and acquaintances, with their knowing looks and persistent questions, made life impossible. Then the phone calls began in the middle of the night. Ted's employer had strong moral convictions about Zachary Brandt's supposed crime and fired him on the spot. The Brandt's had no recourse but to leave town.

Dory pulled her thoughts back to the present. "Santa Fe is wonderful, but I have a job. Just because it's our own shop doesn't mean I can pack up and drive hundreds of miles on a whim."

Ryle's expression said he guessed there was more to her refusal than she was saying. "A pity."

When he'd disappeared into his apartment and closed the door, she looked absently at the proof sheet

Harry was studying, hoping to clear the unwelcome clutter in her mind.

The subjects of the first few shots were a man and woman leaving the courthouse. Dory remembered seeing the story on the news. The man, a small-time politician who'd been caught in the middle of a cocaine buy, was trying ineffectively to shield his wife's face from the cameras.

"What's going on at Koenig Gallery?" she asked, remembering what Harry had said about Ryle's obligation to put in an appearance.

"Didn't Ryle tell you about his showing?"

"No. How long will his pictures be on display?" Dory tried to sound offhand.

"For the rest of this week." Harry slid the picture back into its envelope. "I'll look in for a few minutes every night while he's gone and give patrons of the art a shot of the old charisma."

"You'll charm the socks off them." Megan leaned forward to bestow a kiss.

"I'd better go inside too." Dory sighed. "Congratulations again on your book."

Ted had eaten already, so after her bath Dory finished the leftover Waldorf salad before taking her place at the worktable. She tried to concentrate. But her heart wasn't in it.

Today had been a huge mistake.

Would anything be the same at Sherwood Forest after Ryle decided he was bored with desert scenery and took off for greener pastures? Given the danger of his presence, she should be counting the days. Instead, she couldn't help but worry how she would feel when he was gone.

Needing to prepare for the convention, Ted didn't go to the shop for the next few days. He had to pack his folding booth, prepare samples for trading, as well as price items earmarked for sale. At Wilda's insistence, his obsidian carving of a horse and rider was entered in competition, and needed last-minute attention.

Waiting on customers kept Dory too occupied to allow for moping. But Sherwood Forest felt desolate without Ryle, even for the short time he'd be gone. Now and then she'd think of something she would have liked to tell him—just to hear his rich, unselfconscious laugh. Wasn't that a clear sign she'd blithely stepped off the edge of good sense?

"When I come back," Ted told her, as she was leaving for the class she taught twice a week at the recreation center, "I'll make the rounds of the car lots with you. Together we'll run down a good deal."

"Since when do you know anything about cars?"

"Are you serious? Your mom could tell you a few dozen stories about the heap I drove while I was in medical school." Ted's tone lost its color when he mentioned his ex-wife, something he seldom did unless he was off guard. But gallantly he pushed ahead. "I kept that old fifty-six Chevy together with Band-Aids."

As Dory mentally searched for something to distract him, she spied a yellow suitcase and matching overnight bag next to the telephone stand.

"Wilda's going to the gem show with me," Ted said, guessing the reason for her puzzlement.

"Since when is she interested in such doings?" Dory knew the answer before she asked. Wilda's interest would have been in sumo wrestling, if it involved Ted. Gradually the woman was filling in all the corners of his life, and if he didn't act soon, he was going to have a difficult time separating himself from her.

"If you have problems with the car while I'm gone, ask Harry to chauffeur you. He's an obliging young man."

"I've made it this long," Dory said. "I can make it a few more days."

"I wouldn't place any bets on it."

She wouldn't have either. For now, she was getting through one day at a time, and that night, at least, the aging car transported her safely to her destination.

The class went well, with the students enthusiastic for the polymer clay projects she'd introduced the week before. But her favorite student, a teenage girl who reminded her of herself at that age, had botched a pendant, and was on the verge of tears.

"Your design was remarkable, Kim," Dory told her truthfully.

"So why did it turn out so awful?"

"Once you learn exactly how much to work the clay without overworking it, you'll be ready to start over."

"You think so, Miss Brandt?"

"I know so."

Without thinking, as Dory left the parking lot, she

turned left, instead of right. The Koenig Gallery was only a few blocks away, she thought, easing into the flow of traffic. Seeing the emotions of disaster victims caught by Ryle's camera might reinforce his negative side in her mind. He was out of the city. What better chance than this?

The gallery had neat green-and-white awnings and a display window with easels, holding photographs of two men and a woman, along with times and dates of the showing. One of the men was Ryle, in a pose Dory had seen in a magazine write-up.

One side of his face was in shadow, making his features look sharp. He wore a black shirt and pants that made him look thin, and his hair was shaggier than he wore it now. Inside, greenery spilled over a stone planter. On a white-clothed table lay an open book and a feather-tipped pen for visitors to sign. Dory walked past without pausing, and followed an arrow pointing to the Haggard display.

Where was the crowd she'd anticipated?

"Dory?"

Haltingly, she turned toward Ryle's voice and saw him, devastatingly handsome in a superbly tailored black suit. It was the first time she'd seen him in anything but casual attire, and the sight almost took her breath away. Only the not-yet-healed scratch on his cheek hinted at anything less than perfection.

"Where is everyone?" she managed.

"The Koenig closes at ten on Thursday."

Dismayed, she glanced at her watch for verification. "I came directly from the center. I didn't realize it was so late."

"To what do I owe this honor?"

Quickly she picked her brain for a practical answer. "Harry mentioned your showing. I was in town and decided to see it."

He nodded his understanding. "You thought I wouldn't be here."

"As I said, I was already . . ." Dory broke off as the words evaporated.

"You had nothing better to do?" He continued toward her.

She scowled, not appreciating his humor. "You're part of the Sherwood Forest family. Your accomplishments are our accomplishments."

"Good answer."

What did he mean by that? "Didn't you plan to stay over in Santa Fe?"

"Only if you were with me." He glanced toward the other room. "Let me show you around; then you can drive me home."

"Didn't you bring a car?"

"Harry dropped me off. I expected to take a cab."

This development was working against everything she'd decided about keeping away from him when he returned, but what choice did she have?

Chapter Eight

"Impressive," Dory pronounced after Ryle had escorted her through the main room, their footsteps echoing on the marble floor. As they stopped before each neatly matted photograph he'd given a brief history of the shot, as he might have if he'd been conducting a tour for more than only one.

Missing were representations of fires, plane crashes, and car smash-ups. Instead there were cactus flowers, displays of the sun on rock formations, and rain-slick sidewalks. Innovative angles and lighting effects gave what might have been mundane shots significance, and captured the tone and beauty of the land.

"I expected something . . . different."

His eyes seemed to darken. "The theme here is the character of Phoenix and its environs."

In an attempt to cut unruly thought processes off at

the pass, she fixed her attention on a depiction of an extravagant sunset. The man who'd walked the streets of Justice with her stood beside her now, and the knowledge was debilitating. ''The lucky people who attended tonight got to meet the star.'' She cringed. Had she actually said that?

''I don't think I'd qualify as the star. I'm sharing the limelight with three others and their takes on the same theme.'' He pointed. ''We continue in there.''

''Oh?'' She'd assumed from the posted bio at the end of the row that she'd come to the end of his section.

Dutifully, she followed, but after only a few steps he turned abruptly and wrapped his arms around her. ''Isn't this what you expected when you came tonight? To take up where we left off in Justice?''

''How could it be?'' The air around them crackled with tension. ''I didn't expect to see you.''

''Harry didn't tell you I was back?''

She pulled free, brushing nervous fingers across her forehead. ''We didn't leave off anywhere, Ryle. What happened, happened. We were overcome.''

''We certainly were,'' he admitted.

''By heat and sun,'' she explained, putting more distance between them.

''That too. One thing bothered me, though. When we were with Megan and Harry later, you seemed to have regrets about spending the day with me.''

On the wall in front of her was a collection of charcoal sketches. The subjects were cacti, Gila monsters, and trees with bare branches. If she continued to stare at it, Ryle would sense her insecurity.

"It was your imagination." She forced herself to meet his eyes with her own. The impact was debilitating.

"Was it?"

"Yes. Anyway, this isn't the time or the place." Her gaze moved to the show window, where a man and woman were looking at the display. "People are outside, watching."

"I'll fix that." Ryle stretched out a long arm to click off the lights.

"Don't," she protested.

"We don't need illumination to talk. You were saying . . ."

"I was about to say . . ." Again she lost her train of thought as she felt herself being pulled in two directions. "That actually there is no time or place for us, Ryle. We're too different."

"Isn't difference what makes it exciting?" he countered.

"That's not the difference I meant." Full-color images of their last time together flitted through her mind, and she felt herself weakening.

His eyes shimmered as he started toward her again, and an uneasy laugh bubbled in her chest.

"What?" he questioned, with his characteristic half smile.

"You. Us." She closed her eyes briefly. "I feel . . ."

"You feel what?"

In that moment of anticipation, as she remembered the wonderful pressure of his mouth on hers, and ached for it again, she was perversely reminded of a scene from one of the many vampire movies she'd watched as she was growing up: a brainless heroine standing transfixed as Dracula approached and slowly sank his teeth into her throat. Everybody in the audience was wondering why she didn't try to escape.

Now Dory knew the answer.

"Dracula," she murmured, through parched lips.

Ryle's jaw dropped comically. "You're comparing me to the bloodthirsty count?"

"I only meant . . ."

"I can live with that." Closing the gap between them, before she could protest further, he caught her feverish lips with his, and the memory was new again. His fingers danced at her back, and he pulled her closer, still closer.

"Did you bring the plastic bags?" a crackly male voice called, in crashing intrusion.

"I thought you did," another man said.

Startled, Dory pushed Ryle away, her eyes wide. "Someone's—someone's here."

"I forgot about the maintenance crew," he whispered.

"Maintenance crew? Will they come in here?"

"In about four seconds. Give or take a few."

"Maybe we left 'em in the broom closet." The voice was sharper, nearer. "Lemme go see."

"They'll wonder why we're standing in the dark," Dory said, anguished. "This is . . . embarrassing."

Ryle grinned. "I'll handle the workmen. Wait here."

"You hear something?" There was silence as the workers in the outer office listened.

"Naw. Lookit this mess. Coffee cups. Cookie crumbs. You'd think it was a bunch of kids."

"What are you going to do?" Dory whispered.

Ryle held out a restraining hand. "I'll lead the workers to the other room. When I do, you slip out the door."

"They'll see me."

"Not if I distract them." He grinned. "I'll meet you at the end of the block."

"What a waste," one of the men was saying. "They pour coffee and leave most of it in the cup."

"Gentlemen." Ryle cleared his throat as he approached the two men and held out one hand. "I'm Ryle Haggard."

"The guy who took the pictures? I was told you'd be long gone."

"I like to visit my work when nobody's around."

"With the lights off? Got any identification?" The heavier-set of the two men waited.

Ryle pulled out his wallet and handed it over. "Did either of you see a portfolio? Brown?"

"Nope." The man glanced around.

"Can't say I did," answered his fellow, wheeling a scrubbing machine toward the room where Dory stood.

Ryle barred his way. "Would you mind looking for it?"

"I got a schedule here. Leave your phone number on the desk."

"Actually, I think I left it back there." Ryle pointed.

The man looked suspicious. "Those rooms were closed off tonight."

"I'd appreciate your help." Ryle pulled a bill out of his wallet and pressed it into the man's hand. "Let me give you something for your trouble."

"Do they serve anything here besides coffee?" one man whispered to the other, when Ryle crossed over to a Chinese screen, pretending to look behind it.

"Wine, I think."

"That explains it."

"That way, gentlemen," Ryle reminded them.

As they shuffled off, Dory eased the door open. Though she could still hear him holding forth about the importance of his missing portfolio, the way was clear.

Snatching up her handbag, she made a dash for the street door. Safely on the sidewalk, she sped to her car. Five minutes later Ryle appeared, and she reached across to let him in.

"I feel as if I'm driving a getaway car," she told him.

The car sputtered when she turned the key, but didn't otherwise react. Again she tried, and again it sputtered. Then it shivered and died.

"Uh-oh."

"I could look under the hood," Ryle suggested after a moment of silence. "And maybe kick the tires."

"If that's the extent of your automotive know-how, I don't think it'll help." She tried the engine again, but nothing happened. "Never mind. I belong to the auto club. They'll be here in fifteen minutes, once I give them a call."

"Fifteen minutes?" Ryle leaned toward her and brought his lips an inch from her right ear. "Any idea of what we can do while we wait?" His voice was husky.

"They'll be here fifteen minutes *after* I call them," she repeated, courageously pushing aside temptation. "At the same time, I'll telephone Dad and let him know what happened. He'll worry."

"Curses, foiled again." He let his head rest on the back of the seat.

Dory sighed. "Maybe the man from the towing service will let us ride in the car while it's being towed."

Ryle made a circling motion with his index finger. "I don't know if I could stand the excitement."

"Come on, Haggard," she said philosophically, reaching for the door handle. "Let's find a telephone."

When Dory woke the next morning, Wilda was in the kitchen packing a lunch so she and Ted wouldn't have to patronize the stands at the gem show.

Dory pulled on a pair of white chinos and a knit shirt before fastening her hair at the nape of her neck with an elastic band. A smile touched her lips and remained. She'd be alone for the next few days. But then, Ryle would be on hand to keep her company. The idea was fraught with delectable possibilities.

"Morning, baby," Ted said when she came into the kitchen. He put the picnic basket on the counter. "I was beginning to think we'd have to leave you a note. If Ott comes by, which I don't think he will, tell him

I'll be back Monday. Don't get in an argument with him.''

"No argument. I won't open the door.''

"I was hoping Ryle would have developed those pictures before we left.'' Wilda tore off a sheet of plastic wrap to cover the potato salad. "I want one for my new wallet.''

Dory's smile froze. "Ryle took pictures?''

"At the shop yesterday,'' Ted said.

Why hadn't he said anything about it, Dory wondered, and why had he chosen a time when she wasn't around?

"I thought you vetoed the idea of pictures.'' She held her voice even.

"They were just a few candid shots, honey. It's for a series he's doing on area craftsmen. He's already photographed a woman who specializes in pottery, somebody else who interprets pictures in the clouds, and—''

"We made it clear that we didn't want publicity.''

"Everybody wants publicity,'' Wilda corrected her. "If you have a professional willing to make a gift of that publicity, you'd be foolish not to take it.''

Ted gave a little shake of his head as if to tell Dory not to worry. "It won't be a very good shot. I had my glasses on.''

"I like you in glasses,'' Wilda said. "You look distinguished. That reminds me—have you seen my sunglasses?''

"I think you left them in the car.''

"I'd better check,'' she said. "I can't take the glare.

I see orange and green rings around everything for hours afterward.''

When she'd left, Dory tugged at her father's sleeve. ''Why did you let it happen?''

''He took shots of Ted Brandt, owner of a shop for rock hounds. Brandt not only has a hairline that's rapidly receding, but he's allowed himself the benefit of getting out of shape.''

Dory rubbed the back of her neck. ''Dad, if you give a man like Ryle something to work with . . .''

''Nobody cares anymore, Dory.'' Ted's tone was uncharacteristically sharp. ''I'm telling you it'll be all right.''

Dory decided not to push. The damage had already been done, and there was little point in ruining her father's weekend.

''Can you manage the store while I'm gone?'' he asked.

''I've done it before.''

''Sure you won't go with us?''

Wilda would love it if she tagged along. ''No, thanks. Somebody has to hold down the fort.''

''I guess you're right.'' Ted patted his pocket to make sure he had his key. ''I stuck two paper bags under the counter for people who are supposed to come by and pick them up.''

''Everything will be fine and dandy.''

She hadn't lied, she assured herself, as Wilda's chatter faded away and all was quiet, except for the sound of a leaf blower someone was using across the street. Everything *would* be fine and dandy. But not until she'd thought of a way to get her hands on Ryle's pictures.

Chapter Nine

The weekend was busy at the Rock Place. Then a man came in as Dory was about to close, and delayed her an extra twenty minutes without even buying a candy bar. Usually she wasn't a clock watcher, but she'd devised a scheme to handle Ryle, and was eager to put it in operation.

Too nervous to eat, she showered and donned a sleeveless shift with a print of white butterflies. She teased curls over each ear, and fastened the rest of her hair back with combs. After dabbing mascara on her lashes, she vetoed, as overkill, the idea of eyeshadow, and walked primly to Ryle's door.

His expression said that she'd caught him in the middle of something. Two high-intensity lamps were trained on his worktable, and it was covered with looseleaf notebooks and other paraphernalia. He held a magnifying glass, like the one Sherlock Holmes used, in his left hand.

"You invited me to see you in action," she reminded him.

"I didn't mean—that is . . ." He looked uncomfortable. "Wait a minute."

Through the partly open door, she could see his shadow as he stooped and tossed, hastily putting the room in order. He looked sheepish when he appeared a few minutes later.

"I wasn't expecting company." Dashing as he'd looked in the silk tie at the gallery, this was how Dory liked him best, in jeans and a T-shirt.

Mentally she kicked herself. His appearance was the last thing she should be thinking about. "I don't care about a little dust and disorder. Besides, we'll be in your new darkroom."

"When we finish we'll come back here. To discuss what you've learned."

"I'm only satisfying my curiosity," she said. "I don't expect to put any of it to use."

"You never know."

She didn't argue, but she knew well enough. Once Ryle was out of her life, she doubted that she'd ever want to look at a camera again.

"What happened with the car?" he asked, trailing her down the walk.

"It's in the shop."

"How did you get to work this morning?"

"My bike."

"You should have given me a call. I'd have to given you a ride."

The darkroom had changed. The windows had been fastened with shutters. The sills, along with other exposed wood, were a sleek gray-blue. The file cabinets had arrived the day before. She'd seen the cardboard packaging in the trash bin.

There was a coffeemaker and a minirefrigerator, not to mention a long table next to the sink, with basins to hold chemicals. Lines for drying pictures had been strung from hooks attached to the walls.

As Ryle worked, with only a dim red light for illumination, he explained the procedures, actually making them understandable. In spite of herself she was fascinated, especially when the photographs he'd taken in Justice sprang into sharp images.

"As you can see, your shadow worked. The long dress and the wide-brimmed hat were especially effective."

She nodded, musing that she could have been one of the Justice ghosts, destined to walk the twisted roads forever.

"Care for a copy of any of these?" Ryle indicated the pictures he'd clipped to his line.

"Yes, thank you." She pointed to one taken at the cottage whose porch had caved in with them, resulting in Ryle's slide down the hill.

His eyes caressed hers briefly. "You can see a part of our hillside."

Their hillside.

Brushing away idyllic thoughts, she zeroed in on her reason for being there. "What about the shots you took of Dad?" She tried to sound casual.

"I'll dig them out for you." He seemed pleased at her interest.

Crossing to the central cabinet, he pulled out a drawer and withdrew two manila envelopes. The drawer faces were painted bright colors. The one he opened was yellow; she'd have to remember. In one of the envelopes was a sheet of pictures taken at the shop, each about an inch square. Ryle sank down beside her and waited as she studied them.

Her pulse settled back to normal. Her father was right. With his glasses on, and bent over the counter, he wasn't recognizable, except to those who knew him as the owner of the Rock Place.

"Those aren't bad," Ryle was saying. "But this is the one that captures the man."

He reached in the other envelope and slid out a five-by-seven that took Dory's breath away. It was Dr. Zachary Brandt—a bit older, a bit heavier, but entirely recognizable. He wasn't even wearing his reading glasses.

"I caught him off guard. People get self-conscious being under a camera's scrutiny for a while, and it shows."

"Very nice," Dory managed hesitantly.

"Two copies here. One for you, and one for Wilda. She's been hounding me."

So she had the pictures in her hands, but more could be made. "Is the negative in the envelope too?" she asked, then added, in case he might suspect her motives, "I might want to have some wallet sizes made."

"I'll do it. How many do you want?"

"You've already done enough."

"I don't mind. I keep the negatives separate."

He thunked his knuckles on the green drawer, second from the bottom, section one—indicating that this was where he kept what she was after?

"You must have collected thousands of pictures over the years. How do you find what you want?"

He opened the top left drawer. "This is the master file. We can dispense with it when I've learned to locate what I want via computer. Harry's driving me up a wall, filing everything both alphabetically and numerically."

"He has a different file number for each shot?"

"Right. These are cross-indexed, with subjects, dates, and locations."

Dory nodded, taking mental notes of the number written in black marking pen on the envelope he'd shown her. A metal bar with a place for key insertion protruded half an inch from the facing. A simple click of Ryle's thumb would erase her chances of accessing the negatives.

"Next time I'll show you the enlarger." He turned away without pressing the lock. "And how we manipulate a less-than-perfect exposure."

"I'd like that," she said, shaky with relief. "I still don't see why you wanted a picture of the shop."

He waited while she stepped outside, then pulled the door closed. "As I said, there's a good human interest piece in it."

"You're a photographer, not a writer."

"I'm capable of stringing words together."

"Doesn't taking pictures keep you busy enough?"

"A lot of reasons. One, for example, is the writer

they've assigned me for an article on pets who've saved their owners' lives. The woman is a walking ice cube who doesn't like people. They sense it immediately and don't supply any information but the essentials.''

Unlike Ryle Haggard, who could charm the uncharmable, and loosen the lips of the unloosenable? ''Will you write your own photo essays on your new job?''

''*If* I take the job, you mean. Yes. Not trying to get rid of me, are you?''

''Why would I?''

''To get your storeroom back?''

''Hmm. I hadn't thought of that.''

''Being able to write my own captions and stories is one of the perks that could convince me.'' He looked at her obliquely. ''Have you eaten?''

''Not yet.''

''I saw Ted and Wilda hit the road this morning. So why don't I throw something together for us? Unless you'd rather eat out.''

''I don't think so.'' She needed to shut herself in her own apartment and collapse. ''How about a rain check?''

''I don't give rain checks, and why shouldn't you want to eat? I'd be doing all the work.''

''When you put it that way . . .'' She let the rest of her sentence hang. If they spent the next hour or so together, she reasoned, he might not put two and two together when the negatives featuring Ted Brandt turned up missing.

As he clanked pans and ran water back at his bun-

galow, all the while whistling something unrecogniz-
able, Dory thumbed through a scrapbook of pictures
taken when he was a child. In one shot, a Ryle of
about ten was playing catch with a tall man who was
probably his father. Even then it was easy to see that
he'd grow up to be smashing.

Dinner preparations didn't take long enough for her
to start a second album. After browning meat and on-
ions, Ryle had merely emptied jarred sauce in, and
served the resulting mixture over supermarket ravioli,
but the effect was tasty. This, with shredded romaine
lettuce, a few slices of tomato, and bottled Italian
dressing, made the meal, along with glasses of ruby
red wine.

As they ate, he talked again about the writer who'd
been assigned to him on too many stories, and the chip
she had on her shoulder. They'd done an interview
together, with a group called the Hard Knocks.
Though the possibilities were enormous, as far as he
was concerned, the resulting piece had been merely
passable.

Dory talked about her jewelry classes and how
much she enjoyed helping students develop their talent. "Most of them don't get an ounce of encourage-
ment at home. People don't think of making a career
out of art. They'd rather their kids took computer
classes."

"So you know what I was up against when I said
I wanted to take pictures for a living."

Togetherness surrounded them as they finished eating, and performed the kitchen cleanup, reminiscent of
the last time they'd washed dishes together. Then re-

tiring to the living room once more, she opened the album and asked about people, times, and places.

"My parents had the proverbial marriage-made-in-heaven," he said. "They had their disagreements, but I can't remember either saying anything really hurtful to the other. It's the way a marriage has to be, or why bother?"

Was his attitude about "perfect marriage" the reason he'd remained single so far?

"I'd better get back," Dory said regretfully, as the pauses between their comments lengthened. She'd accomplished the first part of her mission, and it was time to depart, before she got sidetracked. "Dad might call."

"He would have called already," Ryle reasoned, his fingers smoothing her shoulder. "The answering machine would have picked it up."

"I interrupted you at your work," she insisted, concentrating on her escape. "Shouldn't you get back to it?"

"I don't feel like working anymore tonight."

"How many times have you had to work when you didn't feel like it?"

"Not tonight. What we have here is an occasion. You and I together. Miraculously not trading insults."

She smiled shakily.

"No sun beating down on our backs. Little chance of the roof collapsing." He lowered his head to give her the full impact of his gaze. "No maintenance crews to break in. I'd call that an occasion, wouldn't you?"

"When you put it that way."

Satisfied that he'd cleared the first hurdle, he allowed his fingers to caress her shoulder, conjuring up more reminders. "Ever think of taking photographs of the jewelry you make? For advertising purposes? To be able to show prospective clients what you've done?"

She nodded. "I always do. Once a piece is out of my hands, I feel so close to it, I'm tempted to ask for visiting privileges. Of course, the camera can't capture the special something each of those pieces has for me."

"Mine can."

"I can't afford your services," she said. "Years ago I saw a layout you did for—I forget the name of the magazine. You had wineglasses arranged on an emerald satin pedestal, silver light dancing on the rims."

"The magazine was *Elegance.*" He seemed surprised that she would have bothered to learn the name of the photographer. "In the name of friendship, I'd be glad to squeeze off a few shots when you want them."

"In the name of friendship," she echoed. "Should I suspect your motives for making such an offer?"

"If I had a mustache," he admitted, "I'd be twirling the ends of it. But on the plus side, I'm very good at what I do."

Dory could vouch for that. "No, thanks. My Instamatic works fine. Now, as I said, I'd better go."

"What about our celebration?"

She pressed the arm of the couch as she rose. "We had a gourmet dinner. Wine. Congenial discussion. Doesn't that qualify as a celebration?"

"Not entirely."

He stood up too, but instead of walking her to the door, he captured her wrists and slowly, slowly drew her close. His hold was tentative. She could easily have slid out of his grasp. It was almost as if he were allowing for that option.

But she didn't—couldn't—even when his breath scorched her lips, and he pulled her arms around him, as if he were making himself her prisoner.

It was no use. Dory hadn't the strength to quarrel with herself. Too caught up in circumstances to evade his kiss, she met it willingly, eagerly, basking in the heady pleasure of the too-long-awaited contact.

"Now," she whispered brokenly, her lips still less than an inch from his, "you've had your good-night kiss."

Strains of a Lionel Richie song floated from Megan's apartment. But it wasn't only another music tape playing. It was a song written for the moment, with the lyrics full of meaning, just for them.

When the phone rang, she should have welcomed the interruption. Perversely, she didn't. Then the answering machine clicked on. Clearly Ryle didn't intend to answer.

"Sorry to call so early, buddy, but Mindy Fox is flying in from LA," a gravelly voice began. "You know how she freaks when the press shows. I need your Nikon and your incomparable know-how at the airport before nine. Check back so I'm sure you get this."

Mindy Fox was an up-and-coming actress who'd gained notoriety because of a supposed affair with her costar. He was married, and his wife was vocal about her opinion of the beautiful homewrecker.

Flashing an apologetic smile, Ryle freed himself and snatched up the phone. After a few minutes of conversation, he came back and put a hand on each of Dory's shoulders. "Talk about bad timing."

"You're going to the airport to see Mindy Fox? Why don't you leave the poor girl alone?" Dory had seen pictures of Mindy on the eleven o'clock news, her eyes glassy as she ineffectively tried to evade reporters.

"We can't expect to agree on everything, Dory." Ryle's face looked volcanic as he censored what he probably would have liked to say. "Rule number one in any relationship is that we respect each other's decisions."

"Respect?"

He scowled at the negative stress she put on the word *respect,* but didn't say anything. He opened a closet door and took out his camera bag. "People become celebrities because they like attention."

"Then why does Mindy try so hard to get away?"

"Privacy—or celebrity. She can't have it both ways."

"Who are you to say she can't?"

He slapped a hand on the dresser top so hard that a pile of change scattered. "I get burned up when I hear these stars with their phenomenal salaries refusing to sign autographs for kids who've been waiting for hours, claiming that all they owe their public is a good performance."

"Isn't it true?"

"Not in my book. If they don't like the attention they get from their fans, let them work behind a perfume counter."

"So you're doing a public service when you badger these people?"

"I have a job to do," Ryle said tightly. "Let me do it."

"By all means, do it."

In those brief seconds, as he considered her, every speck of warmth left his eyes. "I'm not your father, Dory. You can't lead me around by the nose."

Her mouth sagged. "What's that supposed to mean?"

"The poor man tries so hard to please you, it's pitiful. You're a spoiled little kid wanting her daddy to give in to her every whim, and unfortunately, most of the time he does."

"How can you say that?" She gasped.

"Now I have to take a shower." He grasped the knob as if he could rip it away from the bathroom door. "I don't know what hold you have on Ted, but it's obvious you're controlling his life."

"Yes, I have a hold on him," she shot back, not caring that he saw her tears. "A hold called love. But you wouldn't know about that."

His expression was so cold, Dory had to look away first. "Don't forget to lock the door when you leave," he said.

Chapter Ten

" "Enamel jewelry is almost impossible to repair,"
Ted was telling a woman who'd brought in a piece
she'd bought at a swap meet. Shaped like a turtle with
a movable tail and feet, it was charming, but had a
cracked shell. "I'm afraid you'll have to live with the
flaw."

The woman was becoming testy. "If you people
make jewelry from scratch, why can't you repair
something that's already made?"

Dory closed the door between the main shop and
her workroom. Her patience was thin today, thanks to
Ryle's outrageous accusation.

Since their quarrel, they had exchanged hellos in
passing, when passing was unavoidable. Her plastic
smile couldn't have been convincing. But cocky and

thick-skinned, he likely thought her pseudofriendliness was an attempt at an apology.

Now she had to forget it. Taking her sketches out of the drawer, she sat at the table next to the window and tried again to concentrate. The sun was in her eyes. She got up to adjust the vertical blinds, but it didn't help. Each time the bell rang over the front door, her concentration was broken.

Was a small part of Ryle's accusation true? Even if it were, how could he possibly know how difficult it had been for her through the years, trying to protect Ted, to be everything to him, to make up for the emptiness in his life?

Someone laughed, and she recognized the voice of a regular customer who'd come to crow about a cache of rocks he'd bought at an estate sale. He'd heard that Ted won an honorable mention with his obsidian carving, and wanted to congratulate him.

She went back to her sketchpad. One way or another, she had to get her hands, not only on the picture of her father, but on the negatives. Unfortunately Ryle had been working on a project close to home. His lights burned far into the night, and he was back and forth between his apartment and the darkroom.

Once as she stood at her door sleepless, looking to the stars for the comfort they'd provided when she was small, he appeared in his doorway too. Though she couldn't see his features in the darkness, there was little doubt he saw her. Without saying anything, he went inside and closed the door.

Those few times when he was away, Harry seemed to be ever-present. For a while it looked as if the opportunity would never present itself. When it did, she had to ignore the risk and grab it. He might, at any time, make use of the pictures taken at the Rock Place.

Another Sherwood Forest tradition was a barbecue on the last Wednesday of each month. Harry donned an apron on request, and everybody pitched in for the price of the steaks. Megan tossed a salad, Dory baked beans, and Ted bought soft drinks. Grace Ann made guacamole dip, and her beau supplied beer. Wilda, as usual, did dessert.

Keeping out of Ryle's way was easier than Dory expected. He wanted no part of her either, and melted into one discussion group or another, even allowing himself to be pulled aside by Wilda, who'd decided that if she learned the basics of photography, she might go farther in her field.

As she quizzed him about how to avoid distortion when using a wide-angle lens, Harry held forth with a tirade about his French teacher, and the question of why a person should have to learn a foreign language just to get a degree.

Somehow Dory got through the evening, even the inevitable game. But when a replaying of a videotape made at another gathering was suggested, she pleaded a headache and made her escape.

When she'd changed into a stealthier costume—black pants and a sweatshirt—with a flashlight in one hand and a table knife in the other—she crept to the storage room.

As she'd done once before when she'd misplaced

her key, she worked the knife in the crack between the door and the frame, and jiggled the lock free. So far, so good. She stood motionless for a moment, getting her bearings.

"JL three-four-six," she repeated softly, reminding herself of the file number of the picture she wanted.

Having taken mental notes of what was kept where last time she was there, retrieving what she needed shouldn't take long. She wasn't wrong doing this, she had to remind herself. While technically the negatives were Ryle's property, he had no right to them.

The door didn't make much noise when it opened behind her. But familiar with the faint dragging sound, she spun toward it. The lights flashed on.

"What are you doing back here?" Ryle sounded irritable.

"Why aren't you at the party?"

"Megan thought you looked peaked. I offered to check on you." His smile didn't reach his eyes. "You look like a cat burglar in that getup."

He knew why she was here, she thought frantically. He was toying with her.

"You saw a chance to escape without having to watch the home video?" she asked.

"I saw the flashlight beam bobbing around in the dark. What's the story?"

She touched a hand to her forehead. "Are you withdrawing that offer to share your space?"

"Are you accepting it?"

"That's why I'm here."

He clicked the light on and off to demonstrate that

it was working. "What did you hope to see that you hadn't seen already?"

A good question, and one without a sensible answer. "I couldn't remember how much room there was under the shelves you'd added."

"And the information couldn't wait until morning?"

"I've been unhappy with the cramped space in my closet since I took my trunks home."

"How did you get in?" His gaze moved to her hand, and seeing the knife, he nodded. "A woman of many talents. Why didn't you ask for the key?"

She made an impatient clicking sound with her tongue. "Full of questions tonight, aren't we?"

"If you want the trunk moved, I'll do it for you now," he offered.

"No, no. There's sorting to be done. It'll be another few days."

"I'll be gone over the weekend. But Harry's always glad to lend a hand."

"Another out-of-town assignment?" Mentally she kicked herself. If she'd waited a bit longer, Ryle would have been away. She'd have had an uninterrupted run at the negative.

"Didn't Ted tell you? He and I are going on that rock hunt we talked about."

She clenched her fists for control. If he was waiting for a silent-movie reaction to his announcement, he'd be disappointed. "That's a coincidence. I'm going too."

He frowned. "If I didn't know better, I'd figure you wanted to spend more time with me."

"If you didn't know better." Someone laughed, and a car door slammed. Dory waved a limp hand in the direction of the sound. "Dad will be wondering where I am."

"He won't miss you until he comes back from walking Wilda home."

When he took a quick step toward her, she took a quicker step to one side, and Ryle drew a frustrated breath. "I don't intend to pounce on you. Why do you look so frightened?"

"If it pleases you to think I'm frightened, feel free."

"The old animosity is firmly in place, I see."

"What would you expect after the vicious things you said to me?"

"You find the truth vicious?"

"Truth can be twisted to suit the person who's delivering it."

"So it can," he admitted, abandoning an attempted smile. "Your father said you haven't gone prospecting with him since you were old enough to stay home alone."

"All that talk about rocks at dinner the other night piqued my interest."

His visual inspection covered the room, and returned to the hand holding the table knife. "Are you finished here for tonight?"

"All finished." When he opened the door, Dory walked briskly past him.

"I'll have a second key made for you," Ryle called, not following. Was his plan to go back and see if anything had been disturbed? "So you don't have to resort to breaking and entering."

By the time she'd finished her shower, Ted was back and in the kitchen getting a drink of ice water.

"Feeling better?" he asked.

"Much." Dory absently wiped the dishcloth over a small puddle on the drainboard. "Ryle says you're taking him prospecting."

"That I am."

Would there be any point in going over her fears with him again? "If you have no objections, I'll tag along."

He almost choked on his water. "Are you sure it isn't because of Ryle?"

"How can you think that?"

"Maybe because I know my daughter better than she thinks I do." Briefly, he studied her over his glass. "Maybe I know her better than she knows herself."

Never had Dory had this much trouble with a project. The week before, a woman had brought in a necklace that had been in her family for years. She wanted the stones reset with an Egyptian flair.

"I'd like something unique," she said, a light dancing in the dark eyes she'd painted to look like Elizabeth Taylor's eyes had in the movie *Cleopatra*.

She opened a book she'd brought with her and pointed to colored photographs of ancient pieces on display in a London museum. "I want something that might have been found in the tomb of Nefertiti."

"I'll give you a call when the preliminary sketches

are ready,'' Dory had said, already envisioning a number of exciting ideas.

Now those ideas had flown. She'd just scratched over her latest attempt when Ted opened the door and looked in.

''Dinner in ten minutes. Wilda's here.''

What else was new?

''When she called and I told her you were planning to go with us Saturday, she got all enthusiastic and invited herself along. I asked her to dinner so you two could talk about it.''

What a surprise, Dory thought wryly. ''Need any help in the kitchen?''

''You can set the table.''

''The more I think about it, the more excited I feel,'' Wilda said when they were seated around the table. Dory passed the home-fried potatoes, one of Ted's specialties. ''With another girl along, it'll be fun.''

''Hey, we're not talking fun here,'' Ted protested.

''Any objections to fun?'' Wilda wanted to know.

''Not as long as you know we mean business. It'll work better with the four of us anyway. As you know, I like to take two cars, in case of a problem.''

''You and I can drive one,'' Wilda chirped. ''Dory and Ryle can take the other. I'll fix us a feast.''

''Forget the fancy foods. We'll be roughing it.''

''Any point in not enjoying good food while we're roughing it?''

''As long as you don't make any cucumber sandwiches with the crusts cut off.''

"Give me time to think about the menu."

"I hope you have the right wardrobe." Ted forked up two salted and peppered slices of tomato and passed the plate to Dory. Meaningfully, his eyes scanned the lavender shift Wilda was wearing with its neat white trim. "The desert isn't the place for ruffles."

Wilda laughed. "I'm flexible."

"And you're crazy about snakes."

"I won't bother them," Wilda said flippantly, "if they don't bother me."

When the dishes had been cleared away, she and Ted settled down to watch a television show on wild birds. Dory decided to give the zinnias a bit of attention, though she recognized it as a familiar ploy to keep from getting back to her sketchpad.

The day's heat hung in pockets, as if someone had wrapped the whole city in plastic wrap. The hose was badly in need of a new washer. As she turned it on, water spurted in all directions. Ignoring the spray, she finished the job.

"Dory," Megan called from the door of her apartment. "Come inside. I think all that activity's affecting your brain."

Dory turned off the hose and coiled it in place. "Why do you say that?"

"You? Making a trek into the desert to search for gold? Didn't you see *The Treasure of the Sierra Madre*?"

"I'm not searching for gold." Dory accepted the towel her friend handed her, and wiped her face.

"Come out of the heat and explain."

Dory glanced down one side of the sidewalk, then the other. She'd been aching to talk to Megan alone anyway. Lately it hadn't been easy. "Have you heard anything about Ryle's plans?" she asked quietly. "About the San Francisco job, I mean. Is he taking it?"

Megan's eyes grew comically round. "No, I haven't. Why don't you ask him?"

Dory groaned silently, reading her friend's expression immediately, and realizing it meant that Megan wasn't alone.

Chapter Eleven

Harry was sprawled on the newly slipcovered sofa. Ryle sat across from him in the barrel chair. *Why didn't I wait to make sure the coast was clear before I opened my big mouth?* Dory berated herself silently.

"Are you taking the job?" she asked Ryle, attempting to sound as if she'd known all along that he was present.

"You'll be the first to know," he said in a clipped voice she hardly recognized.

"As your landlady, *I'd* better be the first to know," Megan corrected him. "You'll be leaving me with a vacancy."

"I'll send out a bulletin," Ryle said. "To whom it may concern."

"Enough negative talk." Megan clasped her hands

together. "Let's concentrate on my reasons for calling you all here."

Evidently the two men had been summoned as well, to vote on covers for Megan's book, which would go into print in November. After fanning the possible choices out on the coffee table, she sat on the arm of the couch.

"A friend of Harry's has agreed to do the artwork. Here's what he's come up with. Which do you think?"

"What's *Inklings?*" Dory asked, wondering about the black letters scrawled diagonally across the page and ending in several graduating drops.

"My new title. *Inklings.* Like it?"

"I think there's already a magazine with that name."

"A person can't copyright a title." Megan cocked her head to one side, studying the layout. "I could call it *Gone With the Wind* if I wanted."

"Go for it. You might sell a million copies before people realize they've made a mistake." Harry loped to the kitchen for a refill of iced tea.

Dory looked from one drawing to another, pretending that her concentration was on making a decision, and not on Ryle, appealing as ever in white denims and a wine-colored shirt.

"The gray on black is striking," she said.

"One vote for gray on black." Megan made an imaginary check mark in the air.

"Too much competition out there for rack space. You have to grab the customer around the neck and push his face in the book.'' To demonstrate, Harry fastened his hands around an invisible neck. ''I like the red letters.''

Frowning in contemplation, Ryle leaned forward. ''I think you should go with blue.''

''Ted thought the blue was best too.'' Megan rearranged the covers for closer examination.

''Dad would like everything to be blue,'' Dory reminded her.

''You're absolutely right. Men prefer blue. I'm thinking a blue cover will catch the attention of male buyers who don't usually buy poetry.''

Harry frowned. ''I'm a man, in case you haven't noticed, and I liked the red.''

''You're outvoted.'' Megan stuck the covers in a plastic notebook and wound the string around the clasp. ''Now, Dory, explain this sudden impulse to broil your innards and get all gritty-eyed along with the men, who don't know any better.''

''It's something different.''

''Dory's reasons are anybody's guess.'' With that, Ryle rose and pinned his attention on her face for the first time since she'd arrived. ''All ready for the big trip?''

''I'm raring to go.'' She trailed him to the door, not relishing what she had to say next. ''Dad told you, didn't he, that cameras are a no-no? He likes to concentrate on the reasons for being there.''

Ryle laughed without mirth. ''Why do I get the impression that he was following orders?''

''Because women are manipulative?'' She could have counted to ten in the pause that followed.

''Not all women,'' he said in a growl, turning away.

*   *   *

Before sunup on Saturday, when the camper top had been fastened securely in place on the truck, and the list of what was to be taken had been checked and rechecked, the two-vehicle convoy was on its way.

Wearing khaki pants and shirt, Ryle inquired solicitously about Dory's current project. After describing it as if she believed he was interested, she asked about his next assignment and he told her briefly.

With social graces out of the way, they allowed the car radio to fill the silence, as cactus, cholla, and tumbleweed rolled past. How different the atmosphere was from the last time they'd taken a drive together.

"This must be it," Ryle said when finally, after having been on the road for more than two hours, the truck ahead slowed to a stop.

Dory, who had nearly fallen into a hypnotic sleep, sat up straighter. Ted had swerved onto a stretch of gravel that might once have been a road, but was now spotted with gray-green vegetation and spilled rock. The truck dipped and lurched even at a snail's pace that took it up an incline, then between two tall, tapering rocks like upside-down ice-cream cones.

They stopped on the other side of a terracelike stone. Ted directed Ryle to park parallel, allowing them to stretch a canvas between the two vehicles, forming a ceiling.

"Better than the Hilton," Ryle pronounced when it was done, Ted nodded, apparently satisfied.

While the men dug out chisels, picks, shovels, and canteens, Wilda and Dory set up their kitchen.

"If you're game," Ted said, passing out the whistles each was to wear around the neck at all times, to signal with three blasts in case of emergency, "we'll work till the sun gets hot. Then we'll come back and eat."

"Till the sun gets hot?" Wilda echoed. "I hope this is as hot as it plans to get."

"Sounds like a plan," Ryle said with maddening enthusiasm.

"Dory and I will stay here," Wilda volunteered. "I brought a checkerboard and playing cards."

Dory chewed on the words she didn't say. It wasn't that she wanted to go to the site with the men, but she would have liked to have been a part of the decision.

"Good enough." Ted climbed to the top of the table rock, followed by Ryle. "Quite a view, if you gals care to see."

"Don't look now." Ryle shaded his eyes with one hand. "We have company."

"Ott." Ted slapped his hat against his thigh with vehemence. "Confound it."

"What do you suppose he wants?" Dory climbed up to stand next to her father.

"This was the weekend I was supposed to take him and his family. He must have followed. Let me go down and have a word with him."

"Dad, no!"

Ryle caught Dory's arm, almost yanking her off balance. "Your father knows what he's doing."

"Can you guarantee that?"

"Keep your shirt on and wait." He eyed her narrowly.

Glaring, she yanked away from his grasp and watched the scene below.

As Ted approached the other car, Harvey swaggered over to meet him. The conversation, accompanied by many gestures, didn't last long.

"He said we don't own the desert." Ted smiled ruefully. "He's right."

"He makes me nervous," Dory said.

"He has his family with him. He won't start trouble." Ted scratched a place between his eyebrows. "Even though the site isn't far off, we'd better take Lulu. I'd rather Ott didn't follow and get in our way."

"You think he'll try?" Wilda asked.

"Not if he thinks we're going far. He's brought a metal detector, and they'll likely stick close to the truck."

"And the ice chest full of beer cans," Dory added.

Periodically, over the days and sometimes weeks before a dig, Ted always checked out future sites. This one, he'd informed Ryle as they gathered their equipment, was disguised by tangled growth.

"A flat stretch on one side of a steep drop hints at a dumping area for miners of another era. As it happened, they were so bent on finding one kind of treasure, they overlooked another." Ted mopped his forehead with a handkerchief. "I could be wrong. Shall we give Lulu a try?"

Lulu was a desert vehicle he'd fashioned from spare parts. A two-seater, it looked like a giant inner tube on wheels, but had an improvised roof to hold off the sun, and could take hills at a forty-five-degree angle.

"Would you like to go for a walk?" Dory asked when the men had gone, wanting to keep occupied.

Wilda fanned herself with a magazine. "Ted told us to stay here."

"He didn't mean it as an order." Ted and Ryle's time alone wasn't cause for worry, Dory decided. Casual conversation wouldn't be in order. Ted was dead serious about prospecting.

"How about a game of checkers instead?" Wilda asked. "What do you want, red or black?"

Never a fan of board games, Dory could barely muster up the necessary strategy, and Wilda won all three games. Then the woman put a Tony Bennett tape in her cassette player, and they sat, listening to his sales pitch for San Francisco.

"How come your pa doesn't like my pa?" a small voice sounded at Dory's elbow, and she turned quickly to see a towheaded boy of nine or ten. He wore shorts and no shirt.

"Mr. Brandt likes you, honey," Wilda said. "What's your name?"

"Jason Ott. What's yours?"

"I'm Wilda, and this is Dory. Would you like a cookie?"

"Jason!" The woman who strode toward them had sandy hair piled loosely on top of her head. Her thighs were freckled under the hem of her Bermuda shorts. "Get back here with your own folks."

Without saying anything, the boy ran to meet her.

"Put on a shirt," Wilda called after him. "You'll get sunburned."

The woman grabbed his wrist and pulled him along,

muttering something about people "minding their own business."

Soon the Otts' music started—if it could be called that—too loud for Tony Bennett to compete. Wilda turned off her player, then went over to one of the cots to take a nap. Dory propped her feet on the ice chest and watched Harvey and the others set up camp. Before long the smell of roasting hot dogs wafted up to remind her that she hadn't had breakfast.

She was famished by the time Lulu appeared. Both men were so dusty and drenched with perspiration, they were barely recognizable.

"Hot out there." Ted upended his water bottle.

"Find anything?" Wilda asked drowsily.

"Sure did." Ted indicated the burlap sacks in back of the seats. "We'll sort through it after a while."

"Change your clothes," Wilda chided. "You're soaked through."

"Later. For the moment I want to sleep."

"Sounds good to me." Staking out one of the cots, Ryle collapsed, closed his eyes, and lay still.

Fighting the impulse to watch him sleep, Dory put a long-sleeved shirt, confiscated from her father, over her blouse to protect her sensitive skin from the sun, donned her desert helmet, and set off on her walk.

She hadn't gone far when she found herself with company. Jason and another boy, a taller replica of himself, fell in beside her, carrying staffs they'd made from pieces of wood.

"You'll get splinters," she warned.

"My hands are tough," Jason said. "This is my brother, Harvey. What's your name? I forget."

"Dory Brandt."

The older boy laughed. "Dory, Dooreee, Door. That's a crazy name. Why didn't they just call you Window?"

"You'd better go back," she said, hungry for the solitude she required for mental reprogramming.

"We're looking for gold," Jason told her. "Pa says sometimes you pull up a weed and under it is a whole pile of the stuff."

"You could also find a snake," she cautioned.

Harvey Junior hooted. "I'm not scared of snakes. Most of 'em aren't poisonous."

Jason's pace slowed.

"There's no snakes," Harvey Junior insisted. "Quit acting like a baby."

"It's perfectly sensible to be afraid," Dory said.

Harvey Junior laughed. "You think that because you're a girl."

"Come on, Jason," Dory said, exasperated at the prospect of dealing with the boys in her frame of mind, and with the sun burning her back even through her double layer of shirts. "Let's turn back."

"What did that used to be?" Jason pointed to an old lean-to shack with boards slanted almost to the ground.

"Miners might have built it a long time ago to sleep in when the weather was bad."

"It's not big enough for anybody to sleep," Harvey said, catching up. "Their feet'd be sticking out the door."

"Anything's big enough if you're as tired as they probably were," Dory said.

"Let's batter it down to the ground. Yeeee." Harvey swung his stick over his head and made a charge, with Jason tearing after him.

By the time the men stirred from their naps and were ready to eat, the sun had set and Wilda had built a fire, though they didn't need it. Everything she brought was meant to be eaten cold. "We need it to sit around when we tell our ghost stories," she teased.

"I'm fresh out of ghost stories," Ted said.

"So improvise."

The air was cooler now, but the rock slab was like a frying pan. Though the first place they'd investigated hadn't panned out, the men had located a pocket of tourmaline at the base of an uprooted tree. Ryle and Ted took turns relating their experiences as they wolfed down ham sandwiches, coleslaw, and iced tea. Seeing her father so happy almost made Dory glad she'd come.

"So far we've only cleaned out the debris from the floor," Ryle said.

"But there's good stuff in that debris," Ted reminded him. "We brought it back with us."

"We're heading out early in the morning to widen the cavity to make elbow room so we can get at the better specimens."

"Any chance I can see this mine of yours?" Dory asked, deciding that when her father escorted her to the site, she could question him about what had transpired between him and Ryle, if anything.

"Think you can take the heat?" Ryle asked.

"I can if you can."

"Don't look at me." Wilda pressed a hand to her generous bosom. "I'll settle for a game of solitaire."

"No need to take a chance with your fair skin," Ted said. "Even a hat wouldn't help much with the reflection off the sand. A little later this evening, Ryle can drive you over to see what we've been doing. Decide then if you want to make the jaunt tomorrow morning. Think you can manage Lulu, Ryle?"

"It looks easy enough. That's some jalopy you put together."

"It does the job." Contentedly, Ted looked at the sky. "On a night like this, the moon's so bright you can read a newspaper by it. While you're gone I'll give Wilda a chance to lose another hand of gin."

By the time the men had put their finds in categories, arranging them in Styrofoam-lined cases, Wilda and Dory had cleaned up their kitchen area, and Ryle was ready to go.

"Would you like to drive?" he asked Dory. "You like to be in the driver's seat."

She didn't react. "You know where we're going. I don't."

"Ted was right about the moon," he said when they'd taken their second rise, the last so steep she was afraid she'd tumble out backward. "I've never seen a night so bright."

"Are you sure you remember where you're going? How can you tell one place from another?"

"Can't miss the landmarks. See up ahead?" He pointed. "Those round stones, like a pile of cantaloupe? We make a sharp turn. Then on between the rabbit ears."

Ignoring the hand Ryle offered when Lulu finally stopped, Dory climbed out and looked around. "Where's this tourmaline you two are crowing about?"

"In front of you."

"Where?" All she could see was more cactus and rock. There weren't even any telltale signs of Ted and Ryle's having dug all day.

"Keep walking and you'll trip over it."

She stared at a heap of dried brush. "How could anyone find anything under that spiky growth? It'd tear your hands open. Are you sure you aren't lost and don't want to admit it?"

"What you see is camouflage. Yank it away and check. But don't expect any help from me."

Dory thought at first he was joking, but he only stood glowering, like Chavejo. "Why did you bring me here if not to see the mine?"

"Why did you come along?"

"Not for a reconciliation, I assure you." Climbing to the top of a man-size rock, she gazed over the land. "It's strange. No matter what's happening in the rest of the world, the desert is unchanged. It was exactly like this when I was here before. It'll be exactly like this a hundred years from now."

"According to Ted, changes are going on all around us constantly." Ryle climbed up to stand beside her. "You're right in thinking I had a reason for taking you away from the others. I hoped you might be ready to talk."

She looked up at him squarely. "A moment of truth? Thanks, we already had one."

"I'm sorry if I hurt you."

"I recover quickly."

"You weren't upset because I was going to shoot pictures of Mindy Fox. There was more to it. A lot more."

Uttering a dismissive groan, she worked her way down the slope and got into the desert vehicle as a signal that she was ready to go back to camp. But when he climbed in beside her and didn't put Lulu in motion, her words began to flow.

"A few years ago, Ryle Haggard took a picture that caused a stir in picture-taking circles."

He chuckled deep in his throat. "Picture-taking circles."

"You snapped a picture in St. Louis. It got nation-wide coverage and you won all kinds of awards. Maybe you've forgotten. But I never did. The subject was a little girl whose father died in the crash of a race car."

"I'm a photographer. I photograph."

"After that, I followed your career. There were other pictures. Pictures that brought you notice. But the race-car driver's daughter was the high point. Or should I say the low point?"

He glared at her. "If that picture stuck in your craw, why didn't you ask me about it?"

"What could you say? You're a photographer. You photograph." She stared at the trail ahead. "May we go now?"

He gripped the controls with uncharacteristic ferocity. "You've got it."

Chapter Twelve

Lulu inched up a small rise, lumbered down the other side, and inched up again. Then Ryle growled and switched off the motor.

"What now?" Dory questioned sullenly.

He slapped both hands on the steering wheel. "I was struggling along from one assignment to another, not making any headway, when I got the job in St. Louis because the man at the magazine owed my former boss a favor."

"You needed the money." Dory squeezed her eyes shut. "Fine."

"I went out on this assignment, like I did dozens of similar assignments, taking picture after picture of whatever appeared in my lens. A hundred shots to get one salable isn't unusual. When the car crashed, I was shooting into the crowd, not knowing who the little girl was.''

Dory wasn't buying that excuse. ''You knew when you used the picture.''

''Yes. At that time I had no control over my work. The film was handed over to the editorial staff who'd paid for it, along with my services. When I learned about the story, I tried to reason with my boss not to use it, but he wouldn't listen.

'' 'It's a shot in a million,' he said. 'The guy's dead. Your camera didn't kill him.'

''I threatened to quit. I threatened to bust his head, and in the end he had me tossed out of the building. That episode is why I don't squeeze off a single shot these days unless I own my own copyrights.''

He looked so stricken, Dory knew that what he'd said must be true. As he went on, haltingly, explaining what measures he'd taken to suppress the photograph, she was overcome with guilt for judging him without allowing him to explain. Was it that much different from the way people had once judged her father, without proof?

''I'm sorry,'' she whispered.

Still wound up in his anger, he turned the key in the ignition again. ''I didn't owe you an explanation.''

Again Lulu inched along the sand, dipping, climbing, and dipping again. The campfire came into view, and Dory could see the shadows of Wilda and her father against the side of the truck. In minutes it would be too late to make things right. This time she was the one who reached over to turn off the vehicle's controls.

When Ryle looked at her in surprise, she caught his face between her hands and kissed him, investing all her built-up uncertainty in the contact.

"So you didn't know me in another life," Ryle said when it was over, not understanding.

"No, I didn't." She tried to smile, but couldn't, until he smiled first, if a bit grudgingly, and she knew it was all right. "But we can make up for it in this one."

"So, Dory Brandt." He brushed her hair back from her forehead and kissed the place it had been. His fingertips felt warm and gentle against her skin; still they were faintly rough. "Where do we go from here?"

"We could drive around for a while," she suggested, half in earnest.

"And investigate the beauties of the desert at night?"

"Sounds like a plan," she said, already hungry for another kiss.

"Hi," a small voice piped up. "That car's neato."

Their attention was drawn toward two penlights, moving in circles like fireflies.

"Harvey. Jason," Dory managed, fighting back a giggle at the boys' inopportune arrival. "This is Ryle Haggard."

"Hi, Mr. Haggard," the older boy said. "Can we have a ride in your dune buggy?"

"You'll have to ask Mr. Brandt and your folks," Ryle said through clenched teeth.

"Harvey!" A woman's voice shattered the night. "Jason. Get on back here."

"Aw, Mom," Jason whined. "There's grown-ups with us."

"Get back here or you'll wish you had."

"Ted knew what he was doing when he picked a bright night," Ryle said when he and Dory were alone again. "He and Wilda have seen us by now."

"Probably," she admitted "Shall we join them?"

"How'd you like it?" Ted asked as Ryle nosed Lulu into place on the other side of the campfire.

"Better than I dreamed it would be," Dory said.

"Oh, yeah?" Ted looked at Ryle and back at Dory again. "Does that mean you'll to go out and help us tomorrow morning?"

"Nope." She sat down, cross-legged in front of the fire. "I think I'll stay here and help keep the home fire burning."

"Is everybody ready to turn in?" Ted asked, stretching. "Up before the sun tomorrow, remember?"

The four drew lots to see in what order they'd use the bathroom facilities in the camper. Dory was last, so she was able to take her time brushing her teeth and putting soothing lotion on her skin. The others were already in their cots by the time she doused the lights.

Then the yipping began, reminding her of the last time she'd gone camping with her father. It wasn't mournful, as she would have described it before. It was full of joyous celebration of the night.

"Coyotes?" Wilda asked shakily.

"Coyotes," Ted told her. "Without that sound, we wouldn't know we were in the desert."

"I don't know if I can sleep."

Dory wasn't sure she'd be able to sleep either. But it wasn't the yelp of the little desert critters that would keep her awake. It was knowing that Ryle lay sleepless too, on a bunk only a few feet away.

Wilda rose before everyone else, and started preparations for breakfast. Dory heard voices at the edge of her consciousness, but ignored them, until one turned into a scream.

"There's been an accident." Wilda pointed a trembling finger toward a rocky rise about a hundred yards from the Ott camp. "It's the little guy, Jason. The older boys were climbing the rocks and shoving each other. One of them lost his balance and knocked the little one backward."

"The boy fell from the top?" Ryle burst from the camper, buttoning his shirt.

Dory rolled to her feet. "Is he all right?"

"I don't know. Sometimes kids can take falls that would kill a grown person. Ted went over to find out how bad it is. He knew something bad was going to happen, the way those kids were scrambling around before daylight."

"I'll see if I can help," Ryle said, running in the direction of the Ott camp.

"We could flag somebody down on the road and send them for help," Wilda called after him. "Nobody should take a trip like this without a cellular phone."

"You're right about that," Dory agreed.

As they approached, she took a sharp breath. Jason was lying on the ground. His arms were outstretched, and one leg was bent under him. His skin had a bluish tinge. His eyes were closed, but moved rapidly behind his lids.

The woman was kneeling beside him, crying his name over and over. "Jason, look at me, honey. It's Mommy. Jason. Please."

"Get away from him. I musta fell a hundred times when I was a kid. He hears you women wailing and thinks he's hurt worse than he is." Harvey glared at his oldest son, who stood beside him, the teenager with spiky hair who'd come to the Brandt apartment with his father. "You shoulda looked after your little brother."

"I thought he was with Ma," the boy whined, trying to keep from crying.

"Shut up, and get him some water."

"We got some cold grape juice," Mrs. Ott said, wringing her hands.

"Get it," Harvey barked.

The boy's eyes opened briefly. He bucked and began to vomit.

"Everyone get back." Ted threw himself through the circle and dropped to his knees beside the child. Carefully supporting the boy's head, he turned it to one side. "We have to keep him from choking."

"Get outta his face," Harvey snarled, pulling at him. "You got a daughter. You don't know how wild boys play sometimes. He's fine."

"This juice'll fix you up, sweetie," the woman said, moving in with a glass tinkling with ice.

"Don't give him anything to drink," Ted ordered, waving her away.

"What do you know about it, Brandt?" Harvey barked. "People fall and get winded. Let him have that juice."

"Juice is the last thing he needs," Ted snarled, losing patience. "If you care about your son, let me help him."

"Who do you think you are?" Harvey bellowed, his color rising. "He needs to walk around, is all. Get the blood circulating."

"I'm a doctor." Ted regained his position at the boy's side. "I know what I'm talking about, and we're wasting valuable time."

"A doctor. Right," Harvey sputtered, grabbing a handful of Ted's shirtfront to drag him away.

Moving in, Ryle shot an arm between the two men, clearing a path for Ted with one hand and whirling Harvey away with the other. "Do you want your boy to live? There's a good chance he's bleeding internally. Even I can see that."

Harvey's mouth sagged, and he stayed where he was.

"He has a pulse, but it's rapid." Ted reached into Jason's mouth to clear the passage. Shifting his position, he pinched the boy's nostrils closed and began mouth-to-mouth resuscitation.

"What's he doing?" the woman cried. "Isn't Jason breathing?"

"Your son's probably in shock, Mrs. Ott," Ryle said calmly, keeping an eye on Harvey in case he made another move to stop Ted's ministrations. He put an arm around the woman's shoulder.

"Mr. Brandt's helping him breathe, Mama," the oldest boy said. "We saw a film about that in school."

"What if he does something wrong? He could make Jason worse."

"I used to be a doctor, Mrs. Ott." Ted's voice was deadly calm. "I gave up my practice. But I know what I'm doing. Trust me."

"It's okay, Mama. Mr. Brandt's a doctor. Don't worry."

All was quiet as Ted breathed into the boy's mouth again and again. At last, he sat back on his heels and swiped an arm across his forehead. The boy coughed, and his eyes fluttered open.

"Jason," Mrs. Ott wailed.

"You'll be fine, son," Ted said reassuringly. "It hurts because you took a fall. We'll have you at the hospital as quick as we can."

"Hospital?" Harvey echoed, less sure of himself now. "Where're we gonna find a hospital in this desert?"

"Should we go to the road and flag somebody down?" Wilda asked again.

"Ryle, bring the camper as close as you can, and clear it out." Ted tossed him the car keys, and Ryle took off at a trot. "Dory, go with him. Get blankets. Flatten those two cardboard boxes and bring them here."

"What can I do?" Harvey said helplessly.

"You and your son tear boards off that old shed. Keep them in one piece if you can. We'll rig a stretcher. We can't wait for a team."

While Ryle cleared the back of the camper, Ted

rolled towels to place under the injured boy's neck and back and keep him from moving. Hastily he fastened the boards together with rope and padded them with blankets. "Okay. Ott, stand here. Ryle, here. We shift him on a count of three."

"It's okay, Jason," the woman continued when the boy whimpered.

"Ryle, drive as carefully as you can," Ted said when the makeshift stretcher was settled in the truck bed. "We can't afford to hit any bumps. I'll stay in back with the boy."

"Is there room for me?" Mrs. Ott asked.

"By all means. He needs to know you're here."

"What about me?" Harvey looked as if he were about to cry.

"Follow us in your rig. Dory, Wilda, you ride with Ott. There's a medical center twenty-five minutes down the road. It's small. But there are good facilities."

Harvey drove, gripping the wheel, his eyes staring at the camper ahead. Whether his face was wet from the heat or from tears or both, Dory couldn't tell. Fortunately the traffic was light, but several times they had to slow for rough patches in the road.

At last a yellow structure that looked as if it had been made from a child's building blocks, with add-ons extending on both sides of the main building, came into view. Just as a police car with flashing lights turned out of a driveway marked EMERGENCY Ryle turned in.

At the door he sprang out and dashed through double doors that whooshed open at his approach. Seconds later he was back, with attendants and a gurney.

The corridor smelled more of food than medicine. The cafeteria on their left was in full operation. Only a half dozen people were in the waiting room. Some sat answering questions for a woman who typed the answers into a computer. Others stared sullenly at a TV as they waited to be called.

"He's in good hands, Mrs. Ott," Ted said, leading the weeping woman to one of the chairs.

Watching her father's face during the ordeal, as he demonstrated the courage and calm that had made him a great doctor, had shown Dory clearly what she already knew—how desperately he missed his work.

Numb with pent-up emotion, she started outside, needing to be alone, but Ryle touched a hand to her shoulder. "We're going to the cafeteria for coffee. You'd better come along."

As she allowed herself to be led down the corridor, part of her prayed that everyone would be too drained to discuss what had happened. She should have known better. When they were seated around the chrome-and-Formica table with their cups, her father began without being asked.

"The men in my family have always been doctors. Naturally it was expected I'd be a doctor too." He sipped his coffee, not noticing that he hadn't added sugar.

If he'd kept still, the matter could have been brushed aside, Dory thought wearily. Many people took CPR courses. Ted could have said he had only claimed to be a doctor to gain control of a dangerous situation. But Zachary Brandt hadn't been a liar. Ted wasn't one either.

"I didn't have one quality necessary to be a good surgeon," he went on. "To be able to care, yet to leave that caring behind when I came home at night. As time went on, and I had patients beyond the reach of medicine, it became more and more difficult for me to manage my own life. Dory was suffering. My wife. Our marriage."

"A doctor, of all things," Wilda said dully. "How could you give it up? I have a nephew who's in medical school, and it's a monumental struggle."

"It wasn't an easy choice."

"But you made it," Wilda persisted. "Why?"

Dory looked down at her cup, not wanting to read any questions in Ryle's eyes. She wanted to shout at Wilda to be quiet. To say that her father was exhausted and needed to be left alone.

But it had gone too far. All she could do was listen.

Chapter Thirteen

"One of my terminally ill patients died," Ted said quietly. "This was in Los Angeles, where I was born and raised, and where I went to medical school."

"Los Angeles," Wilda repeated numbly, as if he'd said he came from the Casbah.

"Some people assumed I'd deliberately ended her life, because I couldn't stand to see her suffering. Others claimed I did it because she bribed me, by leaving me a great deal of money. None of it was true. But the story made all the newspapers for a while."

"Knowing how strong you are," Wilda persisted, "I would have thought you'd stand your ground."

Ted pushed his cup aside. "I had my family to consider."

"Can we drop it?" Dory managed.

"Drop it?" Wilda echoed. "It isn't as if Ted just told us he used to grow African violets."

Before Ted could answer, Harvey Ott burst in, followed by his wife. He started to say something, but changed his mind, and his wife stepped forward. Her skin was blotchy, and her eyes swollen. She'd put on her husband's sweater, and it hung to her knees.

"I guess you'll be leaving soon, Dr. Brandt," she said. "But first—I . . . don't know how to thank you. Jason wouldn't have had a chance if you hadn't done what you did. We want to pay you."

Ted held up one hand in denial.

"We got to do something." Harvey sniffed.

"Just be there for your boy," Ted told him. "Knowing he'll be all right is payment enough for me."

Silently the group at the table watched as Harvey slid his arm around his wife, and the two returned to the waiting room. Little more was said in the moments that followed. Even Wilda was at a loss for words.

Later, when they'd returned to the campsite, no one suggested staying. No one had the heart for treasure hunting.

"The tourmaline will still be here," Ted said philosophically as he got in the car with Wilda for the drive home. "We'll try again when we can arrange our schedules."

On the way back, Dory and Ryle talked about Jason and how the accident could have been a blessing in disguise. Knowing the dangers now, the Otts wouldn't let their boys run wild.

Ryle talked about an editorial meeting he had on Monday and how much he dreaded it, and Dory sympathized. Neither mentioned what had happened between them in the desert.

Ryle seemed to be waiting for her to say something. But he didn't ask any questions and she didn't volunteer any answers.

Wilda, drained by the trip, had been recuperating since their return. Ryle had been on an assignment that took him away from home early in the morning and didn't bring him back until late.

It didn't matter. The sky hadn't fallen in. The sun rose, set, and rose again as always. Dory's suntouched peach walls and shag rug still comforted her. When she woke in her brass bed to find her eyes resting on the Marc Chagall poster with its storybook images, she felt enthusiasm for the new day.

In the days that followed, she and her father found a low-mileage used car. It had its original paint job—a metallic green—and it drove like a dream. Now she had an out-of-the-city delivery to make, and could hardly wait to test it on a trip that involved more than a few blocks.

When someone knocked as she was doing an inventive gift-wrap job worthy of the brooch she was wrapping, she found herself hoping it was Ryle. If he was free today, he might make the drive with her.

"Aren't you supposed to be at work?" she asked,

trying not to look disappointed when she threw the door open and saw Megan.

Megan walked past until she was barred by the dining room table. ''The proverbial cat is out of the proverbial bag, so to speak.''

Dory raised a quizzical eyebrow. Maybe the girl had just written a new poem and was caught up in her world of imagination. ''What cat? What bag?''

Megan paused for a long moment. ''You know how I do at lunch sometimes. I sit in the park and read, if there's a park within logical walking distance.''

''I know.''

''I get ideas for poems sometimes from the more outrageous newspapers. So I picked one up at the stand outside our building.''

The girl's meaning struck Dory at once, and her backbone turned to ice. ''You're saying . . .''

''The story about Ted rescuing the boy in the desert, and the death of that woman in California. It isn't on the front page or anything, but it's there.''

Dory snatched the paper away and spread it on the table. Breathing hard, she turned the page. There it was. The story, complete with pictures.

''Dr. Zachary Brandt, who abandoned his southern California medical practice fifteen years ago, and disappeared under a cloud of suspicion after the death of one of his patients, surfaced recently in the Arizona desert, where he saved the life of a nine-year-old boy.

''Dr. Brandt and his daughter, Pandora, own the Rock Place, a shop that sells gemstones and equipment for prospectors in downtown Phoenix.''

The text that continued for several columns was accompanied by two pictures. One, dating back to the time of the tragedy, showed Dory between her parents. The other was the one Ryle had taken of Ted at the shop.

Not able to read the rest, Dory ripped the paper down the middle, wadded the pieces, and hurled them in the wastebasket.

"Sorry." Megan gave her a quick hug. "I didn't want to be the bearer of bad news, but better me than . . . I don't know. Take it easy. I have to get back to work."

How could Ryle have done such a thing? Dory fumed when she was alone. Unable to wait until she'd calmed down, she burst through the front door and stormed across the court to hammer on his door.

"How could you?" she raged when he appeared, his moplike hair indicating that she'd roused him from his sleep—after a late night of dirty deeds, no doubt. His shirt was unbuttoned and he was barefoot.

"What did I do now?" He scratched the back of his head.

"I suppose you don't know."

His expression of innocence made her even more furious. "Let me get some coffee and we'll talk about it."

She held out one stiff arm to warn that he'd better not come closer. "You didn't sell a story about my father and me, complete with pictures, to *Suppressed* magazine, I suppose. Oh, no. Not you."

"If I'd wanted to turn that story in," he said after a long moment, "I'd have done it a long time ago."

"How could you have?"

"Easy. The way you acted when I moved in, as if I were Jack the Ripper? I did a computer check on the name Brandt right away, and learned the whole story about your father and the Santa Monica hospital."

She blew her hair out of her eyes. "You expect me to believe that?"

He scowled. "Frankly, I'm beginning not to care what you believe."

"Somebody broke into your darkroom while you were out, and stole the picture you took of my father?"

A look of awareness crept into his eyes—awareness that underlined his guilt. "Nobody broke into my darkroom, Dory. And I didn't give anybody a story about you. Ted is a friend. I wouldn't do that."

"Mr. Nobility." She twisted her mouth in disdain. "I don't imagine that rag paid much for your effort. You sold out cheap, didn't you?"

He made a grab for her, but she stepped back, almost falling into a spiky aloe vera plant. "At least you didn't earn enough money for your betrayal to make the discomfort of living among enemies worthwhile."

"You're calling me a liar?"

"Did you or did you not say that you have complete control of your work now? If so, how could anyone use your pictures without your permission?"

"I wish I knew." He raised his shoulders and lowered them. "I wouldn't worry. That particular newspaper is a joke."

"I'm not laughing."

Incredibly his eyes, alight with righteous indignation, said that he was the injured party. "I've had it with your hysterical accusations, Dory,'' he said tightly. ''Even taking into consideration what you've been through, and the feelings I have for you . . .''

''What feelings? You're incapable of true feelings for anyone or anything.''

''You'd blame me for the Chicago fire if you could manage it. Since our first meeting you've sat up nights inventing dastardly deeds to fasten on me.''

''I don't have to invent dastardly deeds. Your life is made up of them.''

''Go home, Dory.''

''If you have a speck of decency, you'll accept that job in San Francisco, so we don't have to look at your face day after day.''

''Sherwood Forest isn't big enough for the two of us?''

''Not anymore. I doubt that even Megan will try to defend you after what you've done.''

''Go home,'' he repeated, more vehemently this time. ''And don't come back.''

''You don't have to worry,'' she shouted at the closed door, marveling that he was able to turn the situation around and blame her.

Actually, she was partly to blame. She'd known what he was from the beginning. Why hadn't she been prepared for his treachery?

Not ready to put on a cheery face for Ted, she decided to walk to the supermarket. Pounding the pavement might help her work through her rage. They were out of whole-wheat bread and orange juice anyway.

When ˙ she returned, the sound of an argument grazed her ears as she let herself into the apartment.

Wilda had arrived. It was her first visit since the trip into the desert. But she wasn't her usual sunny self. In fact, she'd been crying.

No casseroles or cream cakes sat on the table. No tempting smells emanated from the kitchen. Wilda was wearing an unbecoming flowered shift and looked as if she hadn't combed her hair.

Had Ted chosen this, of all times, to set her straight about her smothering?

"Don't worry, Dory," she said, picking up her handbag. "I'm not staying. You can eat your supper in peace."

"Wait," Ted tried.

"Ask your daughter if *she* wants me to stay." Before Dory could frame a suitable reply, the woman sniffed. "You see?"

"Of course I want you to stay," Dory said, confused by this unfamiliar side to the woman she'd thought she knew so well.

"You mean you'll tolerate my presence as long as I don't stick my nose where it doesn't belong?"

Ted took a deep breath. "Wilda's upset that I didn't tell her about my medical career."

"It's more than that." The woman's voice was shrill. "I've been in shock for days, thinking. For almost two years I've been trotting over here, telling you everything about me from the time I came into this world to the present. You didn't say a single word about a whole different life you had before you met me."

"Wilda—"

"I knew you were still in love with your ex-wife. I

accepted that. But I was stupid enough to believe you were beginning to care for me too, the way I care for you. Eventually you might even decide . . .'' She began to cry into her hands.

Dory wanted to cry too, though she couldn't have said if those tears were for Wilda, for herself, or for her father, who only stood looking helpless.

''Why don't I leave you to sort this out,'' she tried gently.

''Stay where you are.'' Wilda pointed a finger at her as if it were a loaded gun. ''You and your father are a world complete in yourselves. I apologize for coming between you.''

''You're wrong,'' Ted said miserably.

''People who care don't keep secrets from each other.'' Wilda plucked her purse off the sideboard.

''Wilda, I do like you,'' Dory said. ''Maybe I've been too wound up in my own problems to show it. But I'm happy Dad has such a good friend. You've made a difference in his life.''

It wasn't until she'd said the words that she realized they were true. Ted had begun to look forward to each day and what he and Wilda would do together. He no longer stayed home, puttering around the apartment or watching old black-and-white movies on TV.

''That's not enough,'' Wilda said. ''Not anymore.''

Still hurting from her realization that the dark side of Ryle was darker than she'd suspected, Dory couldn't bring herself to batter an argument back and forth.

''Love is trust, Dory. You two will never be happy anywhere or with anyone until you learn that.'' Wilda grasped the doorknob. ''I feel sorry for Ryle. Someone should warn him that he's spinning his wheels, trying to have a relationship with a Brandt.''

Indignation swept through Dory like a tidal wave. ''Don't waste your sympathy on Mr. Haggard.'' She rummaged through the wastebasket and pulled out the crumpled copy of *Suppressed.* ''Read this. Then tell me what you think of a person who pretends to be a friend, then takes advantage of that friendship to earn a few dollars and a dab of recognition.''

Wilda brushed the paper away. ''You can't blame Ryle.''

''Because it's his job to cash in on the misfortunes of others?''

''No.'' Wilda raised her chin. Her eyes were defiant. ''You can't blame him because he didn't sell the story to *Suppressed* magazine. I did.''

An airplane passed overhead, and the roar filled the room. When it was over, the silence seemed very loud.

Dory looked at her father to check his reaction. His face was expressionless. Then she looked back at Wilda. ''How could you do such a thing?''

''Isn't it what you expected?'' the woman asked. ''Isn't that why neither of you chose to confide in me? Because I might blab your secret?''

''Even if we did, you had no right—''

''Learning the news this weekend broke my heart.'' Wilda wiped at her tears with the back of her hand. ''When I learned that the man I love had another life I knew nothing about, I went through the library at work and found the story on microfilm. I was crushed.

No. Furious would be a better word. I had to retaliate. Then I remembered the picture Ryle took.''

"How could you use Ryle's picture without his okay?'' Dory asked.

"Simple. I passed it off as my own. I knew that even if he was miffed, he wouldn't sue me. But I would have done it even if I thought he might.'' She fastened a scathing glare on Ted.

He shook his head. ''I don't know what to say.''

"I'll make it simple for you, Dr. Brandt. Say goodbye.'' She threw the door open and dashed the length of the walkway as if she thought someone would give chase.

Dory followed her father to his room. ''Did you read the newspaper story?''

Ted opened the closet and stared into its depths. ''Anything in it that wasn't in all the others?''

"No.''

"Then why bother?''

"You're right,'' she admitted, realizing for the first time how much Wilda's quilt dominated the room. How many stitches had gone into the star design, not to mention the hundreds—no, thousands—of fabric diamonds, all in shades of blue? ''What do we do now?''

"Nothing.'' Ted yanked the hangers aside. ''I've always tried to protect you from gossip, baby. Moving every time this thing caught up to us so you wouldn't be hurt.''

"So *I* wouldn't be hurt?''

He shook his head slowly. ''Not this time. My life is laid out the way I want it. I'm more content running the shop than I've ever been before in my life, and I'm staying put. You'd better stay with your mother until the talk dies down. If there is any talk.''

Dory sank onto the bed. ''You're saying we moved all those times—over and over again—to protect me? I thought I was protecting you.''

''Me?'' He snorted. ''When it happened, yes, I needed to put distance between myself and the hospital. But the rest of the relocations? No way. I would have weathered the storm gladly if I'd been alone.''

She pressed a hand to the top of her head as if the action were necessary to keep the information from exploding. ''So would I, if it hadn't been for you.''

His mouth sagged. Then when she laughed, he laughed too.

''I'm sure *Suppressed* magazine doesn't have a huge circulation,'' she said, wondering if he realized the repercussions of the article. ''But the item could be picked up by a major publication.''

''So what? All the undercover living never sat well with me. Wilda did us a favor.''

''Unintentionally. How could she claim to care, but leave you open to scandal?''

Ted looked toward the door, as if he were going over in his mind the words Wilda had flung at him. ''If you think about it, you'll understand.''

''I have thought about it.''

Because of Wilda's actions, Dory had attacked Ryle one too many times. She could still envision the fury darkening his gaze and the unforgiving set of his jaw.

''Memories can be a burden,'' Ted said quietly. ''Some of us carry 'em inside our head and never talk about 'em. But it's like the couple ignoring the elephant walking through their living room.''

Dory was an expert on unhappy memories. This break with Ryle would add more, along with bitter regrets.

''Other people stick their memories in old trunks and hope nobody knows they're there.'' Ted opened his top bureau drawer and checked under a pile of freshly laundered shirts.

Dory stared at him. ''You know about the trunk?''

''What was I suppose to think you were carting around all this time? Golf balls?''

''You never said anything.''

''It was up to you, baby, to talk about it when you were ready. The footlocker isn't much. I gather you got it from an Army surplus store.''

''I did.''

''But the trunk? It's a dandy piece of furniture. Your grandmother thought you'd use it for a hope chest.'' Ted laughed. ''In a way it was, I kept hoping you'd put it at the foot of your bed, where you could enjoy some of your treasures when you felt up to it. I wouldn't mind going over a few of those things myself.''

How could they have misread each other so completely? ''You threw them away in the middle of the night. I watched through my window as you carted sacks out to the curb.''

''I wouldn't have if I'd been thinking straight.'' He opened the next bureau drawer and rifled through it. ''Not all our memories were bad, were they?''

''No, they weren't,'' she admitted, thinking of family dinners and holidays. Among her favorite times were those in the winter, when there was snow in Crestline. They'd bundle up, rent a cabin, and ride sleds down the hill. Records of those times were among the snapshots she'd saved.

Ted closed another drawer without finding what he was looking for. "None of the trouble would have hit us if I'd had the courage to stand up to my family about going to medical school. I was about to give it up when I met your mother. She was so enthralled with being a doctor's wife, I hung in there until I was stuck."

Across the court, Megan had turned on her CD player, setting Engelbert Humperdinck into action again.

"You meant what you said about never wanting to be a doctor?" Dory asked.

"I never meant anything more. Later I tried to tell Adele how I felt. She wouldn't listen. She was already at the breaking point when the scandal hit."

Dory swallowed.

"It was for the best. She and I respect each other. But we're happier apart."

Was he saying what she thought he was saying? "You really care about Wilda?"

"What more could a man want in a woman?" he said. "She's pretty and sweet. She's smart and fun."

Wilda was all those things, Dory had to admit. "And you love her?"

"Yep." He opened another desk drawer. "In fact, after I change clothes, I'm planning to go over and ask her to marry me. Any objections?"

"Would it matter if I did?"

"Not a bit," he shot back. "Have you seen my blue shirt?"

She grinned. "The one with the navy stripe is hanging on the back of your door."

"Ah, my lucky shirt." He tore it off the hanger and headed for the bathroom, giving a low whistle. "That woman has one fierce temper. I'll need all the help I can get."

Chapter Fourteen

If Ted could face an outraged Wilda, Dory mused when she was alone, she could face Ryle.

No, she couldn't.

She considered slipping a note of apology under his door, but instead wandered to her room and sat on the bed, her gaze resting on the fairy-tale images in her poster.

"None of the trouble would have hit us if I'd had the courage to stand up to my family about going to medical school," her father had said.

Was her own quandary only a matter of courage? Would Ryle even open the door to her if she knocked?

By the time she'd made up her mind, he'd left. The next day he was gone again—or still. Wilda swept in at four o'clock, with watermelon, cantaloupe, and honeydew slices arranged on a tray.

171

"Nothing quite as refreshing as icy melon on a hot day," she sang out, as if her acrimony of the previous day had been a figment of everyone's imagination. At least one member of the Brandt duo had been successful in setting his life on course.

Dory agreed that cold melons were refreshing, then hugged Wilda, and was hugged back soundly. While Ted went to get the newspaper, Dory set the table with a cornflower blue cloth. Then the three sat down to an early dinner and a discussion of the upcoming December wedding. It would be small, but smart. The honeymoon would be in New York City.

"I've never seen the Statue of Liberty." Wilda beamed. "Then there are all those New York shows. My boss knows someone who can get us good seats to whatever we want to see."

Ted in the Big Apple? Dory couldn't imagine it. But evidently there was a lot about her father she didn't know.

After they'd eaten, needing to talk to someone, Dory left the kitchen cleanup to her father and Wilda, and crossed the court. Megan's door was open, and Harry was stretched out on the couch, watching a wrestling match.

"I've got a cold," he told her, demonstrating with a cough. "Keep your distance. I guess you know, with Ryle leaving, I'm out of a job."

Ryle had decided to take the San Francisco job? Disappointment lay like a block of ice in Dory's middle.

"Where's Megan?" she managed.

"Across the street gathering opinions about her book covers. She'll be back in a minute."

"Do you mind if I wait?" Dory sank onto the wicker chair, willing her heartbeat to steady.

"I could relocate to San Francisco, but there's Meg to consider." Harry picked up a sofa pillow and tossed it in the air, catching it, then tossing it again. "I know she doesn't want to get involved with me because she's older. But I've got a plan."

"What plan?"

His eyes crinkled with merriment. "When we started seeing each other, she was nine years older than me. I aged a year, but she didn't. So it was only an eight-year difference. I figure I'll be older than she is before long."

Dory smiled wanly. "What will you do without a job?" What would *she* do without Ryle? Her throat ached with unshed tears.

"Ryle's talking to a guy who might take me on. It won't be the same—but, hey, I'll be taking pictures, right?"

"Right."

Harry shot her a knowing look. "What's up with Ryle and you, anyway? I've never seen him in such a foul mood."

"All this animosity between people who love each other is outrageous." Megan burst in, carrying her folder of book covers. "Simply outrageous."

"What do you expect Ryle to do?" Harry asked with a show of indignation. "Dory, here, blames him for what happened to Jessica Halver."

"Never mind about that," Megan warned. "She feels bad enough."

Jessica Halver was the little girl whose father died when his race car crashed, Dory remembered, puzzled by the exchange. "How did you know about Jessica?"

"I told Harry how furious you were with Ryle for taking that picture." Megan inspected her lipstick.

"You told him?"

"Harry already knew about Ted from the computer check. So I wasn't giving away any secrets." Megan gave her hair a pat. "What do you think of my pompadour?"

"Fine on a Gibson girl." Harry snorted.

"I thought if my book took off, I should present an unusual image. The turn of the century had some beautiful styles."

"Ryle told Harry what he'd learned about us?" Dory asked, dizzy from her friend's back-and-forth change of subjects.

"I'm the one who does his filing, remember? Only little Jessie's not so little anymore. She's starting Washington U this year. Ryle kept in touch with the family and saw that they got all the proceeds from those photographs he took." Harry tossed the pillow again, and Megan caught it.

"That's not a toy, sonny boy," she said.

Everything was flying at Dory too fast. How could she have been so wrong about so many things? Why hadn't she listened to Ryle's explanations?

"Where is he now?" she asked.

"Ryle? He's at the studio," Harry said.

"When will he be home?"

"That's anybody's guess. They're shooting an ad for Primitif cologne. Sometimes they run late and he stays over. There's a cot."

So he might not be home that night either? The words Dory needed to say couldn't wait. "Where is this studio located?"

"Oh, no, you don't." Harry sat up, shaking his head vehemently. "Even when he's in a good mood, he doesn't like distractions on the job."

"Where's the studio?" she insisted.

"On Evergreen. But I'm warning you."

"Where on Evergreen?"

"Five-six-oh-one, North. Studio C. Ground floor. But hey—"

"Thank you," Dory said, not bothering with good-bye.

No parking was available in front of the studio. During the three-block walk to get there, Dory caught her reflection in a dress-shop window and cringed. At least she could have put on lipstick and pinned her hair back. As usual when she was fretting, it was flyaway and had a wild, uncombed look.

Nobody answered her knock, but the front door was slightly ajar.

The music was deafening. Lights flashed on and off. Cellophane strips hung in front of fans that blew them every which way. On a pile of fake rocks, four bone-thin women dressed in leopard skins and carrying clubs, leaned over a man in a white tuxedo, who sat below as if stunned.

"No, no, no," someone shouted, and a man in a

royal blue shirt waved both arms wildly. "Didn't anybody hear what I said earlier?"

"Ten minutes," someone yelled.

The music stopped, the cave women relaxed, and Ryle walked out of the shadows. His back was turned to Dory, but she knew his movements and the way his hair curled at the base of his neck. He wore loose-fitting tan pants, and the sleeves of his shirt were rolled to the elbow. The women nodded to whatever he was saying and one struck a pose.

Harry was right. She shouldn't have come, Dory decided. Ryle was too busy to bother with a visitor. Especially one as unwelcome as she would be. Now all she could think of was escape.

The front door had snapped shut when she entered, and was now locked. Groaning, she slid through the dark, barnlike room to a second door. Again no luck. Then she saw it: a red light on the far side of the set. Feeling her way along, she finally found the exit and pushed hard on the metal release bar. Blinding daylight flooded across the floor. Sounds of a truck roaring down the alley filled the room.

"Shut the door," somebody shouted.

As Dory tried to comply, her foot caught in an electric cord. A metal box on stilts that held different-colored circles, like traffic lights, swayed and fell with a resounding crash. The man in the blue shirt leaped onto the platform.

"Who is that girl? Hey. You with the hair. This is a closed set. Didn't you see the sign?"

A dozen heads turned toward Dory. She didn't have to look to see if one of those heads belonged to Ryle.

A bearded man in jeans bounded toward her. "You're causing chaos here, sweetheart."

"I was hoping I could speak with—"

"Nobody speaks to anybody." An unlit cigarette dangled from the corner of the man's mouth.

"Get rid of her," the man in the blue shirt yelled. "Let's get back to work."

"Go before I call security." The man with the cigarette caught her elbow none too gently and led her through the door.

Moments later she was in the alley with the truck driver, and a man who was helping him back up to a loading platform. The studio door clicked shut and the boom-boom of the music started again.

"Stand clear, lady," the truck driver bellowed. "We got a job to do."

"I told you it wouldn't do any good," Harry called when she approached the open door again. He was still lying on the couch, with Megan beside him, but the wrestling match was now a black-and-white movie.

"What'd Ryle have to say?" Megan asked.

"I didn't talk to him." Dory leaned against the door frame. "How will he get home if his car is here?"

Harry didn't take his eyes off the TV screen. "He'll give me a ring when he wants me to pick him up. If it's after ten, he'll take a cab."

A commercial came on. A man in a flowered shirt was doing a lively dance while a chorus sang the praises of a new brand of salsa.

"Mind if I watch with you?" Not waiting to be answered, she settled onto the wicker chair.

Megan and Harry looked at each other.

"Uh . . . not at all." Harry indicated a bowl of popcorn on the coffee table. "Help yourself."

Ignoring the obvious fact that they would rather have been alone, she took a handful of popcorn and sat back, her eyes on the screen even if her mind wasn't. The movie they were watching was peopled with white-faced creatures who crawled out of open graves and staggered toward the unsuspecting in nearby homes.

Seven-thirty came. Quarter to eight, and the phone rang. Dory froze while Megan answered, then handed the receiver to Harry.

"Be there in fifteen minutes," he said.

"You have a cold." Dory sprang up as he wriggled into his shoes. "Stay where you are. I'll collect Ryle."

"Forget it." He continued working his shoes on. "He doesn't need another knock-down, drag-out."

"There won't be a fight. I promise."

Megan caught his wrist. "Let her do it, love."

"Yeah?" He looked at her through the slits he made of his eyes. "What's in it for me?"

Dory made a dash for the door while he was having second thoughts, but paused at the threshold. "Where were you supposed to pick him up?"

"At the front door. And hey, don't make me sorry."

Ryle was sitting on the steps, his equipment at his feet, when she drove up. Obviously expecting to see the van, he did a double take.

"Harry wasn't feeling well," she explained. "I came in his place."

He looked in one direction, then the other, trying to decide if he had another option. "It isn't like him to let me down."

"He didn't. He sent me."

"Like I said." For a moment he considered hailing a cab. But then he opened the door, threw his bags in the back, and climbed in. "Nice car."

"Aren't you going to ask about what happened earlier?"

"When you pushed your way in, knocking things over and setting Petri off on a tangent?"

Dory moved into the curb lane and signaled for a turn. "Petri is the art director?"

Ryle nodded his head slowly. "Want to tell me what that visit was about?"

"I don't know." She couldn't. Not like this.

"You don't know why you came to the studio?"

"Harry said you'd accepted the San Francisco job."

"Isn't that what you ordered me to do?" His tone was cynical.

She signaled for another turn. "Are you forgetting California has earthquakes?"

"I can take pictures of 'em."

"It's windy there."

"I'll turn up my coat collar."

"All those hills are bad for your car engine."

"I'll take a cable car."

"Do they still have cable cars in San Francisco?"

"Before this goes any further"—he tapped impatient fingers on the armrest—"aren't you planning to explain?"

Deciding that words wouldn't perform the magic

she needed, she took a deep breath, leaned over, and kissed him on the cheek.

His astonished expression almost made her regret her hasty actions. Almost, but not quite. "That's supposed to make everything better?" he marveled.

"Under the right circumstances it would," she said, determined not to back down now.

"What circumstances are those?" He wasn't going to make it easy for her.

"If you had special feelings for me."

When the light changed, he focused his attention somewhere outside the car window. "Special feelings didn't help me much at our last meeting."

"I'm sorry for accusing you of wrongdoing without any proof," she said softly.

"How many accusations does that make since we met?" He began to count off on his fingers.

"I didn't keep track."

"Good thing. I'd have to start using my toes."

For the next few miles the silence was deafening. It was even worse when they arrived at Sherwood Forest. She turned into the driveway and keyed off the car engine. "I'll help you with your bags."

"Forget it." He pulled his equipment over the seat.

"Then I'll walk you to the door." She tried a smile. "As long as I'm going that way too."

"Suit yourself."

The lights were out in the other apartments. The only sounds came from Grace Ann's apartment, where someone was playing taped Chopin.

"I still think you shouldn't chase people down and

snap pictures when they don't want pictures taken,'' she said as he worked his key into the lock.

"If this is about to develop into another argument, I decline." He turned the knob.

"But I can see your side of it too." She slid inside the apartment before he could close the door.

He did a double take, as if he supposed he'd left her standing outside. "For your information, I didn't accept the San Francisco job. Yet. I haven't made up my mind."

Hope sparked inside her. "Harry said you did."

Ryle didn't turn on the light. "Harry was playing matchmaker. Wanting to get a reaction out of you."

At Megan's instigation. She might have guessed. "Anyway, I'm glad you're staying." Not that it would help her much.

He slung his bags in the corner. "Not everybody settles their problems by running away, Dory."

A ray of moonlight through the blinds struck the little wood carving, making Chavejo's disapproval seem directed at her.

"So . . . I've said what I came to say," she murmured, recognizing her need to exit before Ryle threw her out. Clearly it was all over between them. "You win. I lose."

Unexpectedly, his hand shot out and held the door closed. "This isn't a horse race, Dory. When people who love each other fight, nobody wins."

"Love?" she echoed. "You never said a word about love."

"How does a man say 'I love you' to a woman who's always jumping on him with both feet?"

"I'm not jumping on you now."

His laugh was a snarl. "You expect me to turn on sentiment like a light switch?"

"Maybe not," she admitted, keeping admirably calm, considering the way her heart was leaping. "Would soft music help? Candles?"

His face was still grim. "Hardly."

Had he meant that he'd begun to fall in love with her before she'd shown a side of her nature he didn't like? Or did he mean he was in love with her now, even if he was angry?

She had to find out. "How about cactus, then, a gravel spill, and sticker bushes?" She moved toward him.

He made a clicking sound with his tongue.

"A blazing hot sun and lizards," she continued, drawing the words out, making her voice throaty and seductive. "Dust."

When a corner of his mouth lifted, she moved so close she had to tip her head back to look into his milk chocolate eyes. "Splinters," she went on. "Red ants. Mmmm, sharp rocks."

"You aren't playing fair." A sliver of humor lit up his eyes.

"What were you saying about being in love with me?" She suppressed a giggle.

"Did I say that?"

"Yes, you did. And it works out perfectly, because . . ." *Here goes,* she thought. "Because I love you too. Completely and without reservations."

"That much, huh? When did you come to that conclusion?"

She considered the question for only a few seconds. "When we knew each other in another life?"

He nodded. "So when I arrived that first day, and you were so maddeningly insulting, you were only playing hard to get?"

"What else?" She twined her fingers behind his neck, holding him fast. "Now that we've found each other, we have to make the most of it, wouldn't you say?"

"Making the most of it includes getting married?" he questioned as if she'd suggested the impossible. "Living together for the rest of our lives? You and me?"

She nodded.

"I'd have to give that arrangement some thought."

"I'll wait." Tightening her hold, she pulled his mouth down to within an inch of hers.

"A whole lot of thought," he grumbled under his breath.

But the moment his lips found hers, all her worries flew out the window. At first his kiss was soft and almost mechanical. With lightning speed it moved to something else. Something so all-encompassing that it answered all the questions she had about his feelings for her now, and all those she'd have in the future.

Ryle had made his decision, and it was a good one.